SUBTLE VARIATIONS

AND OTHER STORIES

BOOKS BY MIRIAM KARMEL

Subtle Variations and Other Stories (Holy Cow! Press, 2017)

Being Esther: A Novel (Milkweed Editions, 2013)

SUBTLE VARIATIONS

AND OTHER STORIES

BY MIRIAM KARMEL

Holy Cow! Press :: Duluth, Minnesota
2017

AUTHOR PHOTOGRAPH BY BILL PRICE
BOOK AND COVER DESIGN BY ANTON KHODAKOVSKY
PRINTED AND BOUND IN THE UNITED STATES OF AMERICA

First printing, 2017
ISBN   978-0-9986010-0-7 *paperback*
ISBN   978-0-9986010-1-4 *eBook*
10 9 8 7 6 5 4 3 2 1

The Publisher is grateful to Mara Hart for her careful editorial attention to these stories.

We gratefully acknowledge the generous support of the Lindquist & Vennum Foundation. This project is also funded in part by grant awards from the Ben and Jeanne Overman Charitable Trust, the Elmer L. and Eleanor J. Andersen Foundation, the Cy and Paula DeCosse Fund of The Minneapolis Foundation, the Lenfestey Family Foundation, and by gifts from generous individual donors.

These stories appeared, sometimes in different form, in the following publications: "Caves of Lascaux" in *Bellevue Literary Review*; "Holy Water" in *Jewish Women's Literary Annual*; "Last Wish" in *The MacGuffin*; "The Queen of Love" in *Minnesota Monthly*; "Summer is for People" in *Moment*; "Pocket Full of Posies" in *Passages North*; "Buona Sera" in *The Rake*; "Mr. Dalloway" in *The Talking Stick*.
"Caves of Lascaux" was reprinted in *The Best of the Bellevue Literary Review*.

Holy Cow! Press books are distributed to the trade by CONSORTIUM BOOK SALES & DISTRIBUTION, c/o Ingram Publisher Services, Inc., 210 American Drive, Jackson, TN 38301.

For inquiries, please write to:
HOLY COW! PRESS, Post Office Box 3170, Mount Royal Station, Duluth, MN 55803.
www.holycowpress.org

ACKNOWLEDGMENTS

For keeping me going, many thanks to the Wednesday Morning group: Lois Duffy, Janet Hanafin, Jean Housh, Sherry Roberts and Ann Woodbeck.

With supreme gratitude and affection to Faith Sullivan for her steadfast support and so much more. And to Carol Dines, who understands.

A special thank you to Jim Perlman for creating a home for these stories, and to the Lindquist & Vennum Foundation for supporting this project.

For the gift of time and space, my thanks to Ragdale and to the Noëpe Center for Literary Arts.

And finally, to Bill Price, for everything.

CONTENTS

FOR

JESSICA

AND

NATHANIEL

The Queen of Love

M Y NONNA DIDN'T TAKE THE ASSASSINATION OF JFK AS HARD as she did the breakup of Lucy and Ricky Ricardo. She was inconsolable for days. During her Ricardo Breakdown Period she continued to do the washing and ironing and dusting, and to sit on the edge of her seat at every dinner, waiting for Grandfather to cut into his meat and pronounce it done. But Nonna could cry while she cleaned and broiled, and cry she did.

I was sure she'd gotten over it until one summer afternoon when the two of us were sitting around watching an *I Love Lucy* rerun. I must have been ten or eleven, still at an age when I found it thrilling to ride the bus to her house and hang out with her. Just the two of us. It was one of those fuggy August days when even the noise from the oscillating fan seemed to generate too much heat, and the only thing left to do was bathe in the cool blue light of the TV.

I remember the way she sat in the recliner, knitting a pair of argyle socks, something she could do even with the lights low, as if she didn't need to worry about picking up a blue strand instead of a yellow or

1

red. But that afternoon she dropped a stitch. I wouldn't have known except that she muttered, "Damn," a word I'd never, ever, heard her say. Then she let the tangle of needles and bobbins fall into her lap and she started to cry.

I went over and knelt beside her. "What's the matter, Nonna?" I said, gently stroking her soft, doughy arm. She felt cool and smelled faintly of bread that's rising.

"Look. Look," she stuttered, pointing to the TV.

It was that show where the Ricardos and Mertzes pile into a convertible and drive to California. While Nonna and I fanned ourselves with back issues of the *TV Guide*, they were in that old car laughing and singing, "California Here We Come."

The Hollywood shows were Nonna's favorites. She loved the idea of Lucy and Ricky and Fred and Ethel escaping that cramped little New York City apartment building for the wide-open spaces of California. She thought the Ricardos, and the Mertzes by extension, deserved a life of palm trees, convertibles, and sunglasses. After all, hadn't Nonna improved her life by migrating west? In her case, the move was from a confined village along the ever-changing borders between Poland and Russia to a not-quite rambling suburban Chicago tract home, known as a ranch-style, though it was missing the cattle. Nonna never looked back. Even when Grandfather begged her to travel to Europe on vacation, "in style," she put her foot down. "Old buildings," she'd say. "I'm through with all that." Clearly, the Ricardos and Mertzes were headed in the right direction. West. To Hollywood. Where everything was new.

That's not to say she would have minded had they gone on forever in New York City. It's just that Nonna liked to say, "How can you keep them down on the farm after they've see Paris?" She pronounced Paris the way she thought a true Parisian would say it. Like this: Pa-ree. Los Angeles was just like Pa-ree, only newer.

By the smiles on their faces, the Ricardos and Mertzes must have thought only good times were ahead. But this being a rerun, we knew better. Not that anything tragic would befall them, just the normal kinds of Lucy hijinks that made everyone, especially Ricky, adore her. We knew that Lucy would get to kiss William Holden after an embarrassing encounter at the Brown Derby. We knew that she'd have a hilarious meeting with Harpo Marx. And by then we knew that Ricky and Lucy would go their separate ways.

What I didn't know, until that afternoon, was that Nonna still hadn't gotten over their divorce. She was pointing at the screen with the two couples riding along in that old convertible. And even when that familiar heart interrupted the action for a commercial break, she was still pointing. I wondered if I was about to lose her to Yiddish, something she broke into whenever she was flustered. It was a trait she shared with Ricky Ricardo, only he ranted in Spanish when he popped his cork.

"One minute they're happy," Nonna said, when she found her voice. "The next, pfft, nothing." She snapped her fingers before drying her eyes with the hem of her housedress.

I remember wanting to ask if she thought Lucy had picked Desi? Or had it been the other way around? But Nonna had picked up her knitting, and by the way she dug her needle into each stitch without glancing at the TV, I decided to keep that particular thought to myself.

You see, love was Nonna's stock in trade, something that pipsqueak rabbi completely overlooked when, years later, he eulogized her as "a housekeeper par excellence." What he failed to note was that Nonna was single-handedly responsible for nine marriages, ten if you count the one that she and her friend Gertie Miller had fought over. Neither Gertie nor Nonna wanted to take credit for that particular liaison, which ended in divorce.

Nine. Ten. The point is that Nonna was a skillful matchmaker. Not only did she have an eye for immediate physical attraction, but she knew (with the exception of Andrea Berman and the dentist) when it would stick. All of the couples, knock on wood—which is what Nonna did whenever she spoke about any of them and their impending anniversaries, births of their children, bar mitzvahs— were still married.

Now it occurs to me that Nonna took the Ricardo breakup as personally as if she had arranged it herself. Her confidence had been badly shaken when Andrea and the dentist (I never knew his name) called it quits. Then the Ricardos parted ways. She must have wondered how such a calamity could occur under her watch. Could she have done anything to prevent it? I think she feared that she was losing her touch. Bad timing, to say the least, given that she had the GGs to marry off in a couple of years. This must be what drove Nonna, if not over the edge, to tears of frustration and dropped stitches.

That's what she called us. "My GGs," she would say, looking from one granddaughter to the other, her eyes misting over. Her gorgeous girls. We even began calling ourselves that, believing it to be true.

We used to gather at Nonna's on Friday nights for dinner and a sleepover. Sometimes we'd stay up all night smearing our faces with her Ponds, our lips with her Scarlet Splendor. We'd speak in fake Hungarian accents like the Gabors. Nonna was such a fan of the Gabor sisters that one summer, at the peak of their popularity, she bleached her hair blond and must have imagined she looked just like Zsa Zsa. She did not. She was very pretty, but she was no glamour puss. She was too soft for true glamour, more like a neatly folded stack of white fluffy towels than a gold lamé dress.

We vamped around the living room in Nonna's high heels and slinky slips feeling gorgeous, and Nonna did nothing to dispel our fantasy. When we weren't vamping, we'd sit around the kitchen table playing crazy eights or canasta, listening to Broadway show tunes (Nonna had a fantastic collection,) eating bridge mix from Nonna's favorite pink cut-glass dish, and sipping tea from tall glasses, the way Grandfather liked it, with sugar cubes and paper-thin slices of lemon floating on top. We played, and Nonna talked about love.

Ruthie, the oldest, was fourteen the year Nonna started lecturing us on matters of the heart. Then, in descending order, came Vivian, Pearl, me (Sophie), and Dara, the youngest, who was eleven and a half. (She never gave her age without the fraction.) That's how old we were when Nonna started in with her preaching: "Pretty soon the boys will be picking you, not the other way around." In Nonna's book, the girls were supposed to pick the boys, but let the boys think otherwise.

She never wavered in her conviction that women are smarter than men. "But they should never let on," she'd say. Coy? Nonna invented it. Not drop-your-handkerchief coy. She preferred dizzy spells and, if all else failed, fainting. "But save it for the right one," she warned. If we told her nobody went around in need of smelling salts anymore, she reminded us that if we weren't careful, the boys would do the picking.

Nonna wanted us to get the crème de la crème, the pick of the crop, the best banana in the bunch. I think she imagined her GGs walking down a receiving line of the most eligible bachelors in Chicago, pausing long enough to ask each man a few questions before moving on. It never occurred to her that we all might fight over the same guy, or that not since King Ahasuares picked Esther from a lineup of all the pretty maidens in Shushan has this been done.

Don't think we didn't remind Nonna that she and Grandfather had an arranged marriage, agreed upon by their widower fathers over glasses of plum wine at Grandfather's house in Stashev, the village fifteen miles from the one where Nonna grew up. We'd cut our teeth on that story. Nonna was sixteen, Grandfather two years older. We knew that Nonna had loved a man called Bondit. Given Nonna's thick accent it sounded like a perversion of bandit, and I imagined that she'd once fallen in love with a desperado, and that only by the grace of God, or more specifically, by the dictates of an arrangement, was she lucky enough to escape his clutches and end up where she belonged, with Grandfather. To this day, whenever anyone says to me, "Tell me one happy marriage," I always say, "My Nonna and Grandfather. They were happy."

But there was no arguing with the Queen of Contradiction. "That was then," she'd say, dismissing us with a wave of her hand. "This is America."

Chastened, we'd play a few hands in silence, the only sounds were the shuffling of the deck, the slapping of cards against the red Formica tabletop.

Then we'd remind her of all the marriages she'd arranged (carefully omitting any references to Andrea and the dentist), and she'd flutter that hand again. "You're on your own, girls," she'd say. "Now somebody deal."

In hindsight, I think that between Lucy and Ricky and Andrea and the dentist, Nonna simply got cold feet. The GGs had no choice but to pick. The problem is, she never explained how. "You'll just know," she said, whenever we asked. Then she'd hum a few bars from that *Guys and Dolls* song.

So here's what happened. Pearl, the group romantic, the one who always had her nose in a book, picked Greg. After graduating from college, they lived together for a few years on a communal farm in Iowa. One day, two months after loaning Greg money to buy a share of the place, Pearl came home and found Greg in bed with Cindy, whom he'd apparently mistaken for communal property. He never repaid the loan.

Vivian moved to Portland, where she works as a nurse in a pediatric cancer ward, and lives with an oncologist named Stella.

Ruthie picked Arnie. Though Nonna didn't live long enough to dance at their wedding, she would have held Ruthie up as our shining example. Never mind that Arnie's the kind of guy who sticks his chopsticks in the serving dish, even when he has a cold. A five-bedroom home in Highland Park, with a three-car garage and an eight-burner stove, would have been proof enough for Nonna that Ruthie had picked well.

Dara, sweet Dara, the baby of the group by half a year, never picked. She never even left home, and for years, speculating on the mystery of why not was a favorite family parlor game. "There's something odd about that girl," the family buzzed. But years passed and the fascination waned. Everybody got used to the idea of Dara hanging back, sleeping in her virginal bed, the same way they got used to Vivian sleeping with Stella.

You can get used to almost anything, though I'm still not used to the fact that I'm no longer married. It wasn't supposed to happen. I remember every September on our anniversary, Simon would congratulate the two of us for having survived another year. Then he'd tick off the couples who had split during the previous twelve months. When I tried warning him not to tempt fate, he'd hiss, "That's insanely superstitious." So every year, as he patted us on the collective back, I secretly crossed my fingers and toes.

I felt a pit in my stomach the year he announced, "We've beat the odds, Sophie. We've surpassed the national average." I wanted to tell him that some things should never be said aloud. Besides, I hated to think or us as quantifiable, like a baseball player's batting average, or the Cubs' chances of this being their big year. I wanted to believe there was some magic to sticking together. But I kept my mouth shut and crossed my fingers and toes longer than usual.

Then one day Simon moved out and left me with everything including instructions to clean out the gutters, which he called out as he rolled down the driveway, his Volvo wagon crammed with books and clothes. He left everything behind that couples typically accumulate over two decades. Tables. Lamps. Braided rugs. Ceramic platters. Later, my lawyer said to be grateful, that some couples fight over the pillowcases. But at the time, as I watched his baby blue wagon recede into the distance, I wondered how he could drive away from a life, as if he were doing nothing more than heading off on vacation— one where he intended to change his clothes often and read stacks of books.

After the Volvo disappeared from view, I returned to the house and took off my ring. I considered walking to Lake Michigan and skipping it across the water like a stone, or flushing it down the toilet like a dead goldfish. Instead, I tucked it into a drawer, thinking that someday I might need to sell it.

Then I drove to the cemetery to visit Nonna, the Queen of Love. Maybe I just wanted to rub it in her face. "See, Nonna, I followed your advice. I picked. But pfft. What do you have to say to that?" I told her that Andrea Berman and the dentist notwithstanding, she shouldn't have lost her nerve. And Lucy? She picked. And look what happened to her." Of course I still didn't know whether Lucy picked Desi, or whether it was the other way around. For all I knew, his *abuela* in Havana arranged the bloody marriage. But at that moment, all I wanted was for Nonna to know that picking isn't easy. You don't always know.

Usually when I visit, I set out a picture of the GGs and I place a sprig of bougainvillea on her stone. That was Nonna's favorite, ever since she and Grandfather spent a winter in Los Angeles in a rented apartment near Fairfax Avenue. I imagined her following in Lucy's footsteps, but she said the place was nothing to write home about, except for the bougainvillea growing near the front door. "Red," she said. "Not like a bird. Not like cherries. Not even Revlon can do such a red. When I die, Vivi, that's what I want. Bougainvillea. Otherwise, don't bother. And whatever you do, never bring a carnation to my grave."

That day I felt like bringing a carnation to her grave, though to tell the truth, I arrived empty handed.

Pocket Full of Posies

THERE'S A FINGER BONE FROM THE HAND OF ST. TERESA OF Avila in a church in Spain. The saint's rosary beads are also on display, as is the cord she used to flagellate herself.

Ruth, the checker at Jewel Foods, saw the bone on her church group tour of Spanish cathedrals. While I was getting my money out, Ruth retrieved a picture postcard from beneath the register to show me what she'd seen. She's always been chatty. Lately, though, I sense she's been trying to entertain me, take my mind off things. I'm sorry I told her about my mother. My job. Still, Ruth's stories amuse me and I like her for calling a bone a bone.

At dinner, I told Hugh about St. Teresa. "That can be anyone's bone," I said. "Anyone's beads. Cord."

"Why would they make that up?" he said.

"Because they can? They made up an entire religion. Why not invent the props to go with it?"

Hugh said it would be bad luck to fake the relics of a saint. That was odd, coming from Mr. Precise. He's a calculator of carbon footprints. His job is to determine the amount of energy one uses by say, flying from Chicago to Paris. Then he finds ways to offset such profligate consumption. Suddenly, he's Mr. Superstitious. He'll say anything to contradict me.

❊ ❊ ❊

First my mother died. Then I lost my job. Then while I was peeling butternut squash a man on the radio said, "Cooking is over." I shouted, "Look at me, wise guy! I'm cooking soup." Then the peeler slipped and gashed my finger. I trailed blood all the way across the kitchen floor to the bandage drawer.

At dinner, over squash soup, I told Hugh, "I'm thinking of going to Paris."

"As in France?"

"No," I said. "As in Paris, Georgia."

There is such a place. I found it in a book, *I Bet You Didn't Know*. There are twenty-six cities in the United States named Paris. There's a Paris, Ohio, a Paris, Kentucky, and a Paris, Missouri.

I've been reading books like *I Bet You Didn't Know*, hoping to discover what people do with their loved ones' ashes. At this point, I could write the book. I'd include the story about a woman in Connecticut who wears her son's ashes in a locket around her neck. And I'd mention the man who tossed a spoonful of his wife's ashes into the bouillabaisse he served at a luncheon following her memorial service. I bet you didn't know that!

What I don't know is what to do with my mother's ashes. I told Hugh I wished she'd been buried like my father, who is laid to rest in a plain pine box at the Jewish cemetery on the city's north side.

He was lowered into the ground according to tradition, within twenty-four hours of breathing his last breath. It happened so fast my brother Barnet, who was on a Princess cruise to the Bahamas with his latest girlfriend, couldn't get back in time for the funeral. "There's something to be said for tradition," I told Hugh.

Hugh said, "You've got to do something with her, Vera. It isn't right." He thinks it's time to scatter my mother's ashes. He says she's languishing.

I reminded him about St. Teresa. "If a church in Spain can display her finger bone all these years, why can't I leave my mother on the mantle?"

"Your mother wasn't a saint," he said, and I said, "You never liked her." Then we fought.

❋ ❋ ❋

She arrived by UPS one morning in May, though I didn't know it was her. The package sat on the front hall table for nearly a week awaiting Hugh's return from a conference. Hugh is always ordering something—a widget for his bicycle, worms for his composter, an out-of-print book. I set the package in the pile with the rest of his mail.

"This must be yours," Hugh said. I was washing lettuce for dinner and he was at the kitchen table going through the mail. He held up a small container. He turned it over; shook it. He even pressed it to his ear, as if he were listening for the ocean in a seashell.

"Mine?" I turned off the water, wiped my hands on my jeans and took it from him. It was a tin box imprinted with a pretty floral motif. I said it looked like it might contain an assortment of English toffee. "But who would be sending us candy, of all things?"

13

Then Hugh read aloud from a note that was in the packing box. Before he finished, I tried handing the tin back, as if we were kids playing Hot Potato. Quickly, he stepped away, picked up a penknife and sliced through an envelope. I sank into a chair and cradled the tin. "I didn't expect her to arrive by UPS," I said.

❋　❋　❋

I was staring at the kitchen floor when Barnet called. The dog had just tracked in mud. Hugh had tracked in something he'd picked up on his running shoes. I was thinking I'd have to get out the mop and bucket and ammonia. I'd have to run the water until it was hot, and while it was running I'd think about Hugh carping if I let the water run while brushing my teeth. I thought of how I'd have to put it all back—ammonia, mop, bucket. Then it would start all over—paws, running shoes. I'd about talked myself out of washing the floor when the phone rang. It was my brother. "I want half," he said.

"Things get lost in the mail," I replied.

"Then send them UPS."

I told him about a UPS plane that had crashed outside of Tulsa, Oklahoma. He hung up.

Not long after, I received a letter from a lawyer directing me to send half our mother's ashes to Barnet. Or else.

"Or else, what?" I asked Hugh. "Will they throw me in jail, if I don't comply? I am not going to pack up half of Francine Bernstein's remains and send them to Barnet."

Shall I divide our mother with a measuring cup, the same cup I use to measure sugar and flour? I'd never be able to make another cake without thinking of her reduced to ashes. As it is, I think of her whenever I bake, though she comes to me full-blown. Alive. Recently, though, I made her chocolate cake, the one from the rec-ipe on the Hershey's cocoa box and I knew she was dead. I didn't know it while I was making the cake, but after I tasted it, I told Hugh, "My mother is dead." It didn't taste like the cake she made for all our birthdays. Then I remembered the time Mother said to Chubby Levine, "I thought you were making my sponge cake?" And Chubby said, "This is your sponge cake." Mother thought that was pretty funny, but I thought it was like asking a woman who isn't pregnant when her baby is due.

When our mother got sick, Barnet took control of her finances. When she was in the hospital, he wrote himself a big fat check and flew to Acapulco with his newest girlfriend. Then he bought a Cadillac SUV.

I told Hugh I believe in karma. "Look at Bernie Madoff." Then I rattled off the names of all the other connivers who ended up behind bars. Jeffrey Skilling. Michael Milken. Martha Stewart. That suave Indian who ran a hedge fund. The list gives me hope.

People do split ashes. My neighbor Caroline scattered half her mother under a rose bush, and now brilliant pink blooms are grow-ing over the fence into my yard. She scattered the other half along the trail where she and her mother enjoyed walking. But I can't imagine my mother as compost and the only walks we ever took were up and down the aisles at Costco.

My friend Marsha's family scattered their mother all around the farm. They sprinkled some of her under the clothesline and recalled all the clothes she'd ever hung. They tossed a bit of her near the backyard swing and remembered the way she was always calling,

"Watch out! You'll get kicked in the head!" They scattered her under the peace sign their father had painted on the side of the barn. There was even enough left for a grave. After the minister spoke, they each tossed some of their mother into it. Then they played a recording of her favorite Glenn Miller song, "Moonlight Serenade," while sprinkling some of her favorite food on top of the ashes. Popcorn. Junior Mints. Potato chips.

I told Hugh, "Some families have all the fun."

❊   ❊   ❊

In the beginning, he brought me cups of tea. He made pots of soup, rubbed my neck. Then he stopped. "There's grief," he said. "And then there's something else. I don't know what it is, but it isn't grief."

He said he'd never known me to be so unhappy. He even said it to Caroline, while she bent over her vegetable garden and attacked the weeds with a kitchen fork. He was standing over her, rubbing her dog's neck. I observed them from the back porch, where I'd gone searching for a book. I heard voices, so I went to the screen and there they were. I couldn't hear what they were saying because of a lawnmower off in the distance. Then the mower stopped and I heard Hugh say, "Vera is not happy."

His mother (my mother-in-law) is still alive. Ninety-three years old and mows her own lawn. The other day she spent four hours planting tulip bulbs. "What do you know of grief?" I asked him. "You've never lost anybody." Horrified, I clapped a hand to my mouth.

Hugh gave me a book: *The Grieving Process*, by Dr. H. M. Featherstone. According to Dr. Featherstone, I will react to my mother's death in stages. When I pass through the final stage, I will be ready,

Dr. Featherstone assures me, "to jump back into the stream of life."

My grief, if that's what it is, doesn't comply with Dr. Featherstone's scheme. It comes in waves. It's messy. Unpredictable. Disorderly. I can be driving and suddenly it feels as if someone has dumped four sacks of potatoes in my lap. Once, while stopped at a traffic light, I realized there was no one to tell me to put on some lipstick. No one to say, *Do yourself a favor. Get rid of that old coat.* When the light changed, I couldn't move my foot from the brake to the gas pedal. Cars honked. Drivers yelled. I sat there and cried. Another time, I was on a garden tour when a woman said, "Smell this rose!" I thought she'd said, "Wake up and smell the roses," but then I saw her pointing to a trellis laden with blooms. I pressed my nose to a blossom and breathed in my Nonna's basement, which had reeked faintly of mildew and gas. Sometimes, I can be enjoying a meal and suddenly the food tastes as if I'm sucking on nickels.

The other day, I was out walking and the sight of some late-blooming phlox triggered a sense of despair so strong that I felt my knees buckle. It took all my will to keep moving. I couldn't recall any association with phlox. My mother hadn't gardened. Like me, she set a few pots of geraniums on the front stoop every spring. Yet something about the fading phlox behind a white picket fence made me weak in the knees. Or perhaps it was the weathered green and white striped cushions on wicker chairs arranged haphazardly on the front porch. The place looked like home. Not the home I grew up in, but a home nevertheless. I wanted to go home. Only I couldn't.

When I tried describing the porch, the cushions, the phlox, Hugh said, "Home is where the heart is, Vera." I'd expected him to say, "You can't go home again." Either way, I was sorry I'd brought it up.

17

Is there really such a thing as too much grief, which is what Hugh is suggesting? Perhaps there's a grief gene, expressed in some kink on the strand of DNA that determines all one's other traits. My particulars include: washed out blonde hair; green eyes; short, stubby fingers; broad forehead; a slight bump at the bridge of my nose. No one has ever called me pretty. Interesting. Yes. Also lurking on that double helix that determined I would look interesting, not pretty, may be an over-expressed gene for grief.

My Nonna would have passed it on. Nonna grieved out loud. We'd be sitting around the dinner table—me, my mother, father, two brothers, Nonna—talking about the Cubs, or the stock market, or the tree that fell on the neighbor's car during last night's storm. Everyone would be talking at once. Then Nonna, who'd been quietly minding her own business, would lament, "*Oy*, Lou. Why did you die?" Just as suddenly, she'd sit back in her chair and fold her hands in her lap, like a cuckoo bird that retreats into its clock after heralding the hour. Before long, we stopped paying attention to Nonna's eruptions. Now, if Nonna were alive, I would say, *Tell me about your grief and I'll tell you about mine.* Back then, though, we kept on talking about falling trees, the tanking stock market. Someone always predicted that next year would be the year the Cubs would pull it off.

❋ ❋ ❋

I was spritzing my wrists with perfume at the fragrance bar in Macy's when I heard someone say, "I have become the kind of woman who wears Enna Jetticks."

Crazy, but I thought it was my mother. It's easy to imagine

18

her worrying that she'd become such a woman. She worried about everything. And she was always worrying out loud.

"In my next life," she'd say, as if she were a member of some esoteric Hindu sect, not a reformed Jew who attended synagogue once a year on the High Holy days. "In my next life, I'll be carefree. Lighthearted. I won't give a damn about anything, Vera. Just you wait and see." So it wasn't such a leap to imagine my mother worrying out loud that she'd returned as the kind of woman who wore Enna Jetticks. Old lady shoes, she'd called them.

Not that the voice I heard was anything like my mother's, which was high- pitched and slightly nasal. The voice that carried down the length of the perfume bar was in a lower register. Finishing school came to mind. Summers in Nantucket. Locked jaw. What would such a woman know of Enna Jetticks? For that matter, what does anyone know of shoes that today might only be found on e-Bay?

The woman at the perfume bar who was not my mother had on strappy sandals with high heels and tiny gold buckles that fastened at the ankle. They were fire engine red.

Enna Jetticks were almost always black, though occasionally blue or beige. Most had laces and a modest, firm, broad heel. My first grade teacher wore black Enna Jetticks in winter, beige in autumn and spring. My father's secretary, Bunny Kohlberg, always wore Enna Jetticks, though you'd expect a woman named Bunny to wear a more playful shoe, a strappy red sandal, perhaps. Nobody in my family wore them. My aunts on my father's side—the Gabors, my mother called them—never left the house in anything but high heels. Every night, before bed, they moaned about their bunions and hammertoes while soaking their feet in hot water and Epsom salts.

19

The women on my mother's side wore Capezios or Weejun loafers with knee socks, unless they were off to a wedding or bar mitzvah or a night on the town.

My eye traveled up from the red strappy sandals and followed the curve of the woman's calf to the point where her leg disappeared beneath a gay cotton skirt with a pattern of blowzy pink peonies. "A nice leg," I thought. My mother was always quick to remark on the shape of a leg. "She's a pretty woman," she'd say. "But get a load of those piano legs. Poor thing." Sometimes, out of the blue, she'd say, "You're lucky, kiddo. You've got nice legs. That's nothing to sneeze at." Later, I would study my legs in the bathroom mirror, trying to figure out what was nice about them. Or I'd try to figure out, for example, how the legs of a woman who'd sat across from me on the bus, had anything to do with the legs on my Aunt Vivian's Bechstein?

I spent much of my childhood trying to decipher my mother's remarks. "It was like learning to speak a foreign language," I told Hugh, early in our relationship, when I told him everything.

Turning my attention back to the fragrances in front of me, I spotted my mother's perfume. I dabbed some on my wrist to get a whiff of her heady, floral scent. After she died, I went through her closet, heaped her clothes on the floor and rolled around in them, hoping to soak up her essence. Later, I packed her clothes off to a women's shelter, but I kept her perfume. It's on my dresser, flanked by all the other bottles—Queen among the pawns. I never use it. Sometimes, though, I uncork the glass stopper and expect my mother to pop out of the bottle. Crazy. I know. Crazier still is that the perfume feels more real to me than her ashes, which are still on the living room mantle. How did Hugh put it? Languishing.

I set down the perfume and glanced again at the woman in the red shoes. She appeared to be in her mid-forties, like me. Her hair, a striking white blonde, was cropped short, showing off, to great effect, silver earrings the size of bangle bracelets. Other than a splash of color on her lips, she wore no makeup. She was pretty.

My mother was a bolder kind of pretty, like the peonies on the woman's skirt. Her hair was black. She wore it long, even at an age when most women lopped theirs off, as if they were entering a convent, not middle age. During the day, she controlled her hair with a plastic headband or a silver barrette, but at night she set it loose, like an animal that had been caged for too long. She smudged kohl around her eyes. And she always wore red lipstick, even when she cleaned the house. She played her beauty to the hilt, though she rued her legs, which were covered in a tangle of varicose veins. "Them's the breaks, kiddo," she'd say, as she held out a leg, studying it from this angle and that, while seated on the edge of the bed to put on her nylons.

The woman who was not wearing Enna Jetticks had smooth legs, though my mother would have found some flaw. If I were to say, "She has nice legs. Don't you think?" my mother would purse her lips and give me the stink eye. "Have I taught you nothing?" she'd say. "Look how bowed they are. Wait till she walks. You'll see. Rickets. They were probably too poor for milk when she was growing up. Her father drank the milk money." If I were to say, "How do you know all that?" she'd smile a crooked smile. "How do I know anything? Let's just say, 'I know.'" My mother was a firm believer in her own infallibility.

My cousin Simca called her a witch. "A good witch," she'd say. "Not the kind that eats children who get lost in the woods. Your mother knows things that other people don't know."

"She's just smart," I'd say, and Simca would shake her head and give me a baleful look. "You don't understand. Your mother knows things that nobody can possibly know. Not from books. Not from anything."

"You mean she has ESP?"

Simca sighed. "Oh, Vera, forget I said anything."

If my mother was so smart, why didn't she tell me what to do with her ashes? I read that Peggy Guggenheim gave instructions that she was to be buried with her Lhasa Apsos in the garden of her palazzo on the Grand Canal. My mother, of course, hated dogs. "Why would anyone have an animal in the house?" she'd say. Still.

I considered asking the woman what she would do. But she and her red sandals had taken off. Vanished. Poof. Just like my mother. One day she was sitting up in bed telling me to get a mirror and her lipstick; next day she was gone. Later, when I told Hugh, "She could have given me some warning," he said, "She was very ill, Vera. How much warning did you need?"

Dr. Marks was no help. "Everyone's different," he'd said. "But Francine is remarkably resilient." Then he shrugged, held his hands out in an empty gesture, and said, "Your guess is as good as mine, Vera." While I appreciate a doctor who willingly acknowledges his own limitations, I felt troubled when Dr. Marks turned my mother's prognosis into a guessing game, one that I, an out-of-work teacher of English as a Second Language, might play as well as a medical specialist. Guess how many jellybeans are in the jar! Guess what's behind Door Number Two! Guess when your mother will die!

I glanced down the counter again, but the woman was still not there. I didn't need her advice. I've had enough of that. Simca suggested scattering my mother at Père Lachaise. "Near Jim Morrison's grave," she said. Simca dropped a lot of acid in college and followed The Doors everywhere. As far as I can tell, she's never regained her equilibrium. Even before that, my mother would say, "Vivian must have dropped Simca on her head when she was a baby."

Friends have suggested scattering my mother from a mountaintop. My Aunt Vivian told me about a charter boat that takes groups out to sea. When it drops anchor everyone tosses their loved ones' ashes overboard. It sounded like those Korean weddings where a thousand couples get married en masse. I told Vivian, "That's creepy." She agreed and confessed that her friend got into a fight with a man on the boat because he wore shorts and flip flops, and left his shirttails hanging-out. "Your mother would have turned over in her grave at the sight of him," Vivian said. "That's the problem, Aunt Vivi. Mother isn't in a grave. Remember?" Then I reminded her that my parents had fought the day they were scheduled to buy their burial plots.

My mother's version of the story started with my father peering over the morning newspaper and saying, "Today's the day, Francine." When she said, "The day for what?" he reminded her they had an appointment to check out the plots. That's when she announced her plans for cremation. She reminded him that their tour guide, on the cruise they'd taken for their fortieth anniversary, had informed them that every plot on the Venetian burial island of San Michele had been spoken for years ago. New arrivals are dug up after ten years and moved to a common burial site farther out in the lagoon. "Venice!" Father exploded. "Are you cuckoo? This is Chicago. We have an option on two plots at Waldheim. Nobody is going to dig us up. Ever.

Now go get ready, or we'll be late." Later, Mother confided, "Your father shouldn't have used the word 'ever.' I was already thinking of which handbag to use on our little outing. But the thought of spending eternity with him." She paused. "I can't explain it, but something came over me."

❄ ❄ ❄

Now my mother is on the mantle wedged between a ceramic candleholder from Oaxaca and a wooden doll from an Indian tribe whose identity I no longer recall. The mantle is full of stuff I've carted home in suitcases. A crystal vase from the duty free shop in Dublin. A water jug from a potter at a street fair in Santa Fe. It's all there, in what Hugh calls, "Vera's pantheon of *tchotchkes*." I can pass by six times a day and never see any of it, not even my mother, whose remains are stored in a pretty tin box. Hugh is right. My mother is languishing.

The other day I came upon her while tearing the house apart in search of a cookbook, which I'd mislaid on the mantle. "Hey, Francine!" I said, pretending it really was my mother languishing in the tin box. But my mother was tall and full-figured. She had a presence. People looked up when she entered a room. The last time I saw her, she was sitting up in a hospital bed, telling me to get her lipstick. "Hurry," she said. "The rabbi will be here any minute." I held the mirror for her and when she was done coloring her lips, she said, "Now plump up my pillows, and find a way to dim the light. Nobody looks good in fluorescent."

When the rabbi arrived, I kissed her cheek and said I'd see her in the morning. Now she's in a tin box. "That's pretty weird," I told Hugh. "One minute, she's putting on lipstick for the rabbi, the next she's being vaporized in a sixteen hundred degree furnace, and then pulverized in a high-speed blender. And I'm supposed to believe that whatever is in this tin is my mother? For all I know, it might contain somebody else's ashes. Such things happen, you know."

I still haven't opened the tin. One afternoon, about two weeks after it arrived, I carried it into the living room, sat on the sofa, and poured myself a glass of wine. With each sip I promised myself that before the next sip, I would lift the lid. But I couldn't stop thinking of Pandora.

※　※　※

And then I thought of Lillian and the afternoon I ran into her, on my way back from the *mercado*. This was years ago. Her eyes were red from crying; her cheeks were streaked with blue mascara. Even her hair, which ordinarily covered her head like a protective shell, a blonde, lacquered carapace, had collapsed. "Bobbie died," she said.

Bobbie was a yappy white terrier who had gone everywhere with Lillian. She kept him tethered to a baby blue, leather lead, though sometimes, like a French woman, she tucked him into her handbag. Lillian was from Teaneck, New Jersey.

I hugged Lillian and offered to escort her back to her place, which was also mine. We were both renting rooms for the winter from the Aguados—Rafael and Lolita—who owned a rambling home on a dusty road in San Miguel. Their place was about a fifteen-minute walk from the Plaza Civica and even farther from the bougainvillea-covered tourist posadas that looked like money. Lillian refused my offer. "I took a valium," she said.

Lillian was not the kind of woman who evoked pity. Once,

I'd stopped her in the Aguados' courtyard to ask directions to a *pana-deria* she'd been raving about. She started to explain, then stopped, looked at me, as if for the first time, and said, "If you ever expect to find a husband, you'd better do something with your hair." Still, that afternoon, as she blew her nose into a shredded tissue, I felt sorry for her. I felt even sorrier for Bobbie, though I hadn't liked him. He was an exotic breed, with white extravagant fur that frizzed around him like cotton candy. He yipped and cried on the rare occasions when Lillian left him alone. In the mornings, he chased after Lourdes, the young girl who cleaned our rooms, nipping at her ankles.

After Lillian and I parted, I slipped into a small church and lit a candle for Bobbie. As I watched the flame flicker then bloom, I repented for ever having called Bobbie the Devil Dog, if only under my breath. I also prayed that I would not be punished for imperson-ating a woman of faith, a woman of a different faith, one who had no business standing before a shrine to Santa Rita lighting a candle for a dead dog. Then, audaciously, I crossed myself, following the example of the woman who had preceded me at the altar.

A few days later, I watched through my window as Lillian tended the flowers outside her room, which like mine faced the courtyard. I was waiting to catch her doing something. But what? Sob and fling herself in despair onto the ground? Kiss Bobbie's baby blue leash? Fill his water bowl, which she kept outside her door? Instead, she did ordinary things like press a finger into the flowerpots to test for mois-ture. She deadheaded some marigolds and moved a potted begonia out of the sun. Then she looked around, as if she sensed someone was watching her. Foolishly, I ducked behind the curtain, but she saw me and waved, motioning for me to come out and join her.

When I asked how she was doing, she ignored me and continued watering a Bird of Paradise. I was beginning to think that I'd only imagined she'd beckoned me, when she set down the watering can and said, "Come inside and see Bobbie."

Lillian had a deluxe room. Unlike mine, hers had a kitchen and a capacious living room. "He's over there," she said, pointing to the mantle above the adobe fireplace. The mantle was lined with blue and white ceramic mugs and plates, the kind you can pick up in the *mercado* for a song. I scanned the mantle not knowing what to say. I thought that Lillian had gone off the rails. Then, just as I was about to pretend that I saw her poor mutt lurking amid the crockery, she plucked a shiny object from the mantle. It looked like a tennis ball can that had been sprayed with silver paint. "He's in here," she said. "Bobbie's in here." She held the can close to her cheek and kissed it. "Such a little dog," she said. "And so many ashes. How can that be?"

When I asked what she planned to do with his ashes, she backed away from me, hugged the can to her breast, gave me a fierce look and said, "How did you get in here?"

I don't know what became of Lillian and Bobbie. Perhaps he's still on the mantle. More likely, Lillian took him home to New Jersey. By now, Lillian may be on a mantle somewhere. That all happened so long ago, before I met Hugh and settled down. It happened, as my mother would say, long before moveable type.

❊   ❊   ❊

"A tour bus driver stopped me and asked, 'Are you from here?'" Hugh pauses and looks around the table, gauging his audience. I've heard this story. He told it at dinner the night he returned from his meeting.

27

He's embellishing now. Or else I've forgotten this particular detail—that the driver had an English accent. Perhaps I spaced out when he told it the first time. Lately, he's been accusing me of that. Spacing out. More likely, I received the abridged version, the energy-saving iteration of a story that, either way, isn't worth stopping a dinner party in its tracks to tell. Before Hugh grabbed the spotlight, the guests, eight in all, were talking in little groups. The room buzzed with their chatter, reminding me of my neighbor Caroline's bees. Then Hugh cleared his throat and launched into his story—the unabridged version. When it had been just the two of us, he must have done some mental calculation, the kind he does for a living, and decided there was no need to squander his energy on me. Now he's the SUV he rails against, the energy hog releasing too many hydrocarbons into the air. He repeats the bus driver's question, this time with an English accent. Then he says, "We were in *New* England, for God's sake." He's shaking his head in faux bemusement, signaling that laughter would be appropriate since after all, he had not been in England. He'd been to a meeting of other carbon-offset calculators. They hold their gatherings in expensive, inaccessible venues. This one was on an island. "We were in New England," he repeats, with another shake of his head.

Colin, the lawyer for Hugh's non-profit, is sneaking a look at his watch, and Susannah, the group's web guru, just telegraphed a desperate look to her husband across the table. Hugh, undeterred, is barreling ahead. "I told the driver that I was just visiting. Nevertheless, he said, 'Do you happen to know if John Belushi is buried at the cemetery down the road?'"

The British accent is getting on my nerves. After the guests are gone, I'll say something. *You sounded like Sacha Baron Cohen impersonating a Russian oligarch.* Hugh will groan. *I was that bad?* I'll nod and he'll laugh and I'll laugh, and then we'll finish our nightcaps and toddle off to bed. No. I won't say anything. Not tonight.

He's still holding forth. "Of course, I said that I didn't know where Belushi is buried. But then, get a load of this, the driver said, 'Oh. That's okay. I'll assume that he is.'"

An uncomfortable silence settles over the table. When Hugh told me the story, I said, "Assume? You don't think he actually drove by the cemetery and announced that John Belushi is buried there?"

Now the man seated to my right—I've forgotten his name—hits the rim of his plate with the base of his wine glass, which he has just drained for the third, or possibly the fourth, time. Meanwhile, Hugh's story hovers over the table like an auction item for which nobody has offered a starting bid. I must break the silence. I catch Hugh's gaze and say, "You don't think that he drove by the cemetery and announced that John Belushi is buried there?"

For my effort I receive a withering look, the look Hugh has sent at countless dinner parties, the one suggesting I might not want to pour another glass of wine. Only this look doesn't feel protective. He is reprimanding me for speaking out of turn, for rushing in before any of our guests—his co-workers, dullards every one—has had a chance to speak. Why do I feel as if I've helped myself to the hors d'oeuvres before all our guests have been served?

I return Hugh's look with a shrug, then continue. "It makes you wonder if you can trust anyone. Or any *thing*. I mean, here are all these people, paying good money for a tour, and their guide is making things up. Dare I say, lying?"

In the right setting, my remark might trigger a discussion of trust. Trust in government. Trust in your fellow man. Or woman, I might add, should the conversation take that turn. Who can you trust these days? What can you trust? Can you trust that your government isn't spying on you? Or that your pilot has landed the plane many times before, but not so many that he's too old to be flying? For that matter, can you trust that your husband hasn't fallen for your neighbor, the one who has become a beekeeper? There was something about the way he chatted with Caroline the other day, the way he stood there rubbing her dog's neck while she weeded her tomato plants with a kitchen fork.

But the conversation doesn't turn to trust. Instead, Colin asks Hugh, "Is he?"

"Is he what?" Hugh sounds peeved. It's the tone he reserves for me whenever I challenge him. Once, I suggested that buying carbon offsets is not unlike buying indulgences for absolution. "The rich can pollute, then buy a tree and feel absolved," I'd said. He didn't speak to me for days.

Colin is trying to clear up the confusion. "I mean, is John Belushi buried in that cemetery?"

When Hugh shrugs, the lawyer says, "Well, I suppose you didn't have time to go look for the grave."

It is a statement that can be read either way. Colin may be acknowledging that Hugh had more important things to do. Or perhaps he's suggesting that Hugh lacks curiosity. I'm putting my money on the latter.

I'd asked the same question, more or less. "Did you go to the cemetery?"

"Why would I do that?" he'd replied.

When I said, "Why do we do anything?" he accused me of being "too existential."

"But your little tale does raise the matter of existence," I'd said. "Didn't the bus driver say, 'Are you from here?'"

If the assembled weren't such dullards, I'd try to revive the conversation along such lines. Instead, I hear myself saying, "My mother didn't want to be buried." Suddenly, I'm launching into the tale of how, on the day she and my father were scheduled to buy their burial plots, she announced her intention to be cremated. "If my mother were buried," I tell the assembled, "I could visit her grave. Lay flowers beside it. Set stones on her marker. Instead, she is languishing on the mantle. That's what Hugh says. 'Just leave your mother to languish on the mantle, Vera.' But really, if my mother is languishing, it's her own fault."

Nobody is checking a phone, consulting a watch. I have everybody's attention when I say, "Peggy Guggenheim specified that she was to be buried with her Lhasa Apso's in the garden of her palazzo on the Grand Canal. I bet you didn't know that."

· In one of my V8 talks, the talks I imagine I'd had with my mother when she was alive, I tell her about Peggy Guggenheim and her dogs. Then I say, And you? What are your wishes? Of course, true to form, she replies, *I can't see why anyone would have an animal in the house. I certainly don't want to be buried with one. Honestly, Vera, you take the cake.* Then I explain that the Lhasa Apso story was only an example. *It would just help, I say, if you could tell me what you want me to do. With you.*

But the matter of her ashes never came up. We talked about everything but dying, unless you count the time she said, I suppose

I had a good life. Only in one of my V8 talks did I think to say, *Tell me more.*

❉   ❉   ❉

When Simca suggested Père Lachaise I said my mother never shared her enthusiasm for The Doors. Then the next day, while going through my mother's belongings, I found a satin handbag. Inside, in florid script, a small tag read, Paris, France. It felt like a sign.

The bag has a delicate golden chain to wrap around your wrist. A spray of flowers is stitched to one side. Why does the word posy come to mind? Ring around the rosie. A pocketbook full of posies. Or ashes. I've considered packing my mother in it. But it may be too small, even though my mother, who was forever dieting to lose the same twelve pounds, has been reduced to a mere four pounds of ash.

The satin bag has a small zippered compartment in which I discovered a tissue. My mother's lips are on it, blotted in red. Funny, but that lipstick stain feels more real to me than her vaporized, pulverized remains.

I even found a penny in the bag. A penny for your thoughts. I never said that to her. Not even when she was in the hospital and said, "I suppose I've had a good life." I remember there was resignation in her voice, as if she were telling the butcher, I suppose that rump roast on the end will do.

She'd been sitting up in bed reading the newspaper and I was sitting across from her knitting a scarf for Hugh. I remember dropping a stitch and saying, "Crap." Then I picked up the stitch and finished the row. I never picked up on my mother's remark.

If that had been me sizing up my life, Dr. Becker, the therapist

Hugh found for me, would say, *Suppose? Aren't you sure that your life was good?* Then there'd be a long silence, during which time I would be wondering whether Dr. Becker counted the minutes waiting for me to speak. Or I would calculate the cost of saying nothing. Or I'd try to guess the cost of the shoes Dr. Becker tucks beneath the chair that she sits upon lotus style. Then she would say, *The hour is up, Vera. We'll take this up next time.*

I thought there'd be a next time when I gave my mother a swift kiss on the cheek and said I'd return in the morning. When I asked if she wanted anything from the outside world, she said, "Paul Newman." We laughed. At least there was that. A last laugh.

But I never cut through to her when she had a voice. I never said, *Aren't you sure that your life was good?* Now I have conversations with her in my head. I call them my V8 talks. Hugh thinks that sounds like a summit meeting of the Western Allies. "It's nothing like that," I told him. I asked if he remembered the commercial where a man drinks a sugary beverage, then slaps his forehead and says, "I could have had a V8!" That's what I do. I slap my forehead and say, "I could have said this when she was alive. I could have said that."

There were so many times when I could have said this or that, like that day in the hospital when she read the paper and I knitted. I remember at one point, she said, "Get a load of this." Then she tossed the paper aside. "Oh, never mind." She sighed and flopped back into the pillows. "The Republicans exhaust me. I won't miss them."

"Are you going somewhere?"

"Honestly, Vera. You take the cake."

"You said, 'I won't miss them,' implying . . ."

"Implying nothing. When those bums are voted out of office, I won't miss them. End of story."

Now, in my V8 talks, I say things like, *There's more to the story.* Sometimes I ask if she's afraid. Predictably, she says, *Afraid of what?* To which I reply, *You know. Dying.* And then she says, *Who said anything about death?*

That's how it would have gone, even if I had talked to her when she had a mouth.

Now I imagine her walking into the store where she bought the satin handbag, selecting it from among all the others, one prettier than the next. What was she wearing that day? What day? What was I doing when she walked into that shop? And where is it? So many questions. Why didn't I ask them when I could?

When I told Hugh I was going to Paris, I didn't tell him that I planned to find the shop, though by now it's probably a Benetton or a Gap. But if it's still there, I intend to find it. Then I'll stroll in with my mother dangling from my wrist by a golden chain and I'll say, *I bet you didn't expect to see this place again, Francine. Did you?*

Holy Water

VIVIAN SUGARMAN LOOKS OUT THE KITCHEN WINDOW, SUR-
prised that the ducks that had nested by the pool all spring
have returned. Not until an arm emerges lazily from the water, followed windmill-style by the other, does she understand that what she
briefly mistook for the pintail feathers of a mother duck is actually a
woman's hair, fanned out around her head as she does the back crawl.
It's Frances Hartley.

She can't recall inviting Frances for a swim. Or had Frances
issued her own invitation and she'd acquiesced. Though she can't
recall that, either. Frances at least could have rung the bell and
announced herself. Then what? *Actually, today isn't the best, Frances.*

Vivian should march outside and say just that. Instead, she pon-
ders the salad greens for this evening's dinner while praying that
Frances will simply slip away. Then she spots the chaise lounge,
cloaked in a brilliant towel, repositioned to take advantage of the
late afternoon sun. Frances is here for the long haul. Vivian glares
at her friend who is now treading water, energetically scissoring

35

her arms overhead. It's a move she likely learned at one of the spas she frequents. Frances is Vivian's oldest friend, yet except for their age—54—the two have little in common. Frances loves to shop. She embraces, with evangelical fervor, the most outrageous fad diets. She is conversant with Oprah's books. The two share history, though. Frances is the closest thing Vivian has to a sister. But even a sister shouldn't show up uninvited.

Earlier this summer the rabbi and his wife had come for dinner. Over drinks, the rabbi announced that he'd like to borrow the pool.

"Borrow my pool?" Vivian asked. People borrow books. Even cars. But how does one borrow a pool?

"For a conversion," he said, sounding almost taken aback by Vivian's surprise. In a more measured tone, he explained what she'd already known—that tradition required a convert to attend the mikvah, a ritual bathhouse. "But all we really need is a still body of water. Your pool will do," he said, so matter-of-factly it would appear the matter was settled.

A body of still water. That she hadn't known. She laughed. "My pool? A mikvah?" though she'd never been to one, she imagined a dank, cavernous, mysterious place far removed from her verdant yard with its shimmering sapphire pool.

"We make these things up as we go along," the rabbi said, dismissing her concern with a priestly wave of the hand. "You understand, don't you *tsatskeleh*?"

She did not. The idea of purifying oneself for conversion, or before marriage, and then monthly at the end of each menstrual cycle, struck Vivian as quaintly Old World. Superstitious. Irrational. Even crazy. Crazier still in a suburban backyard swimming pool.

Soon Vivian and the rabbi fell into a routine. He'd bring the convert to her house and following brief introductions he'd say: "Go with Vivian, *tsatskeleh*. She'll lead the way to the *cabaña*." Always, he pronounced the latter with an exaggerated Spanish flourish.

Her pool became a revolving door through which young women—Carolyns, Jennifers, Heathers, names as interchangeable as their faces—emerged as Jews. Add water and *voilà!* Instant Jewess. Vivian wondered if their initiation shouldn't be more challenging, demand more sacrifice, at the very least a visit to the dank ritual bathhouse? Joining so troubled a tribe should require something more than a couple of classes in the rabbi's study followed by a dip in a kidney-shaped pool.

Yet Vivian faithfully played her part, escorting the Jennifers to the powder room, standing outside the door while they changed into bathing suits. Poolside, as they slipped out of their cover-ups, she turned away with unexpected modesty. It wasn't the flesh that unsettled her as much as the vulnerability of these naïfs, child-women swept up in the drama of so unorthodox a production. Mikvah. *Cabaña.* Yiddish. Spanish. How could they know that their baptism in a faux mikvah was the wild invention of a notorious rule bender? The rabbi, a scholar, a renowned free thinker, presided from the pulpit in bespoke Italian suits. One Yom Kippur, the holiest day of the year, he shunned his priestly white raiments in favor of a tuxedo (to his congregants' dismay). He poured French wines at his seders.

Things spun out of control. Lately, she has considered ending her arrangement with the rabbi. In her mind, she's ended it so many times that she's beginning to believe she actually told the rabbi:

The *cabaña* roof caved in. The truth is, Vivian can't even walk out into her own backyard, march up to Frances and say, *What are you doing here?*

Frances. There she is, hoisting herself up the ladder, shaking her head like a wet dog.

Vivian makes a deal with herself. If Frances isn't gone by the time she finishes with the salad, she'll march outside and . . . And what? She couldn't even buy the greens she'd desired. "We don't carry that," the clerk had said. That. As if the word was distasteful, though she believes that soon enough iceberg will stage a remarkable comeback. The clerk suggested frisée, which she finds bitter, and the texture off-putting, like eating feathers. "Perfect," she'd replied, cowed by a young man with an extraordinary tattoo snaking up his arm.

Cowed by Ray, too. He'd arranged the dinner. Without consulting her. He even suggested the menu: rosemary chicken; baby purple potatoes, their cost inversely proportionate to their size; cheesecake. The salad.

Vivian has stopped collecting Ray's shirts at the cleaners. She has begun mismatching his socks. The other day she changed the pillow-cases on her side of the bed only. Yet here she is preparing the dinner *he* had promised to cook for Dan and his fiancée.

Until recently, Dan had been married to Frances. They'd wed three weeks after Vivian and Ray. The couples had even exchanged vows in the same ballroom—a room overlooking Lake Michigan at the Belden-Stratford Hotel. To the delight of Vivian and Frances, already friends for a decade, a foursome quickly developed. That was thirty years ago. Now Ray assumes that the foursome, albeit slightly modified, will continue. He has accused Vivian of being stubborn, unyielding. He claims not to understand her discomfort around newly configured couples, of which, lately, there have been too many. Divorce has infected their circle of friends; there have been a few deaths, too.

It's true. She has trouble accepting the new arrangements. She forgets the replacements' names. "The understudy," she'll say to Ray. "What's her name? You know, that little interloper with the extraordinary cleavage."

She can't deny the arguments in favor of moving on. Still, does it have to appear so easy? Does she have to fall in line so quickly? She wonders if Ray could take up with someone new, leave her, the way Dan left Frances? Just like that. One day, Dan returned home from a run and announced that he wanted a divorce. The next morning, Frances was sitting in Vivian's kitchen and between bouts of tears said, "He stood there dripping sweat on the clean floor, pacing, head bowed. He said he's suffocating." Frances blew her nose. "I had no idea."

Now, Vivian tells herself. *March out there now and tell her.*

But she is distracted by the sight of Frances tugging at the elastic leg band of her swimsuit, trying to tuck in the escaped flesh of her plump buttocks. She doesn't know I'm watching, Vivian thinks. Suddenly, it occurs to her that she might learn something new about her friend of forty years, though she already knows too much. She knows, for example, that Frances didn't get out of bed for three weeks after Dan left, except to stumble to the bathroom or accept deliveries of the improbable items she'd ordered by phone. Lavender bath oil. Leather pants. A tea kettle that whistled the opening bars of *Für Elise.*

Now. Go out there now. Vivian starts for the door, then pauses as Frances removes a compact from her straw bag. She watches as her friend freshens her lipstick, bares her teeth to check for smudges, peers up her nostrils. Frances chucks herself under the chin and frowns. Then she anoints her body with tanning oil, sinks back into the chaise and closes her eyes.

You've got to tell her. Dan is coming to dinner. With Effie.

She remembers the morning Frances called. "Effie," she rasped. "Her name is Effie." Then she hung up and Vivian dropped everything and drove straight to Frances's house.

Go out there. Now. Tell her the dinner was Ray's idea. Tell her about the mismatched socks; the shirts still at the cleaners.

She looks out at her friend, then at the pool of standing water, the same standing water where Effie became a Jew. Now Frances rolls over onto her stomach causing the carefully encased buttock flesh to escape. And Vivian, who had turned so modestly from the disrobing Heathers, is transfixed.

Place Cards

I HAD ONLY EVER SEEN HER IN BLACK AND WHITE, IN A SNAP-
shot taken on the occasion of my Aunt Vivian's wedding. Still,
I knew her lips were the color of bougainvillea; she would smell of
frangipani. Her name was Shelita and she had sat for Diego Rivera.

Shelita was married to my Nonna's brother Paul. He's the sibling
who scattered to Mexico. *Scattered* is Mother's term, which makes
our relatives sound like billiard balls.

From Stashev, Nonna and Grandfather scattered to Chicago, by
way of Toronto and Detroit.

Nonna and Paul's youngest brother, Samuel, scattered to South
America, where he spent years working odd jobs. After Grandfather
sponsored him, Samuel scattered to Las Vegas. "Poor Schmooly. He
was a gambler with little luck and littler sense," Mother would say,
with a touch of pride. She was fond of him, perhaps because he had
enormous faith in a golden future.

But the brass ring went to Shelita, whose life changed simply by
staying put. She had just finished her shift as a telephone operator
and was waiting for a bus when Paul showed up. He'd just come from

meeting the man who sold him the textile business that would provide the kind of money that procures portraits by great artists. Mother told the story the way some people spin tales of Hollywood starlets discovered waiting tables at dusty roadside cafes. "Life is so random," she'd sigh. "Poor working girl runs into man fleeing for his life. Next thing you know, she's posing for Diego Rivera. Anything can happen. Even Schmooly spins the right numbers once in awhile."

Shelita's photo appears to have been snapped by another wedding guest, one impatient for the hired photographer to work his way through all the tables in the room. In it, four gilded women are seated in a semicircle. Behind them stand three men in dark suits and ties, their shirts bright and starched as the table linens. The table glitters with water goblets, wine glasses, heavy cutlery. The women, in soft dresses that plunge modestly at the neckline, glitter too.

Only Shelita appears in profile. Her hair is pulled back in a tight chignon, fully exposing her nose, beaked like an Aztec warrior goddess. Her lips are not visible, but I knew they would be painted purple or plum, some color I'd never seen on the lips of the other women in my family. She must have turned her head just as the photographer coaxed smiles from his reluctant subjects. "Say cheese!" They would have balked, told him to hold his horses, the real photographer was on the way. He would have frowned as he looked through the viewfinder and said, "What am I? Chopped liver?" And so the women smile, their carmine lips parted, exposing perfect teeth. The men sport intoxicated grins. Perhaps Shelita smiled when she turned and looked away.

"Something glittered and caught her eye," Mother said. "A necklace or a pair of earrings. Perhaps a dress that she coveted. She wanted so much."

❋ ❋ ❋

The family was abuzz for weeks with the news that Shelita and Paul were coming to town. Queen Elizabeth, who had recently visited the United States, didn't create such a stir, though Mother and Nonna and Aunt Vivian had plenty to say about the fur coat the Queen wore to a college football game in Virginia. Grandfather was a furrier and those three had convinced themselves that, by extension, they knew every trick of the trade. "Weasel fur," Mother shuddered. "Cat," Vivian sneered. When he heard them arguing over the Queen's coat, Grandfather said, in his heavily accented English, "Ach! The way you talk. Dond be such damned fools." Nonna, who was forever saving things "for good," suggested the coat might be fake. "Maybe the Queen didn't want to wear real in such a crowded place." Only after Grandfather left the room did they agree he had a point. But the next day, those three were at it again, bickering over the authenticity of the pearls Her Majesty had worn to the top of the Empire State Building.

The Mexicans were like visiting royalty. They were movie stars in Technicolor to our Black and White. I remember greeting them with a curtsy and then backing away. Later, when Mother said, "What the hell was that about?" I explained I'd seen curtseying on the Queen's visit to New York. "Shelita's no queen," she snapped. "She was a telephone operator when Paul met her. She took part-time jobs on the side making sweaters and cakes." When I said, "I thought you liked her," she said, "I do. But next time, a simple 'hello' will do."

There was a lot to do before Shelita and Paul arrived, and Mother, who once had visited them, established herself as an authority on everything Mexican. She said their house, a meandering old Spanish

43

colonial, was "a regular *palacio*," with so many rooms she lost count. There was even a room for storing the silver, and maids to polish it all. Coffee urns. Bowls. Cigarette boxes. Candlesticks.

She said Shelita and Paul's sons learned English from a British nanny and were tutored in Latin and German and chess by a Hungarian émigré whom Uncle Paul had befriended while in flight. Once, the tutor drove the boys to the mountains to see snow. The youngest packed some snowballs into a cardboard box and was inconsolable for days after they melted on the drive down. The boys had Bar Mitzvahs. They were baptized, too. On Sundays they attended Mass with their mother. A crucifix hung over every bed in the house. "There's a lot of schizophrenia in that household," Mother said.

The Mexicans weren't crazy. They simply experienced life in another dimension, one in which you could worship different gods and appreciate fire and ice in a single afternoon. They conjured heat and chili peppers, parrots and hibiscus, rose-colored stucco, painted tiles. They had a maid who stood by the breakfast table waiting to refill the coffee cups. And they owned a painting by Diego Rivera— the portrait of Shelita—that hung over the living room mantle.

We called them "the Mexicans" to distinguish them from "the Canadians," our relatives on Grandfather's side. The Canadians never created a stir when they came to town, perhaps because we spoke the same language and suffered the same winters. Like us, they were in Black and White. The Canadians, if I thought of them at all, con- jured argyle socks and cardigan sweaters. They dressed in gray and smelled of strong tea and damp wool. They were bureaucrats and accountants, schoolteachers and clerks, though Grandfather's old- est brother was an ophthalmologist.

* * *

On any given day, you could eat off Nonna's floors, which was the measure of cleanliness by which she judged a woman's ability to manage a household. In the days leading up to the Mexicans' visit, Nonna flew into a tailspin, surpassing her own exacting standards. She sent rugs to the cleaner, hired a window washer, and found somebody to dust the blinds. She had the living room sofa cleaned, though it was always shrouded in plastic. She roped me into polishing the hideously gnarled feet of the rosewood breakfront. Not trusting anyone else with the task, she got down on hands and knees to scrub and wax the kitchen floor.

Mother, who had a relaxed approach to housecleaning ("reaction formation," she liked to say), poured her energy into studying Spanish. She listened to *Six Weeks to Conversational Spanish* while fixing dinner and during the time she ordinarily reserved for her soap opera. The house was plastered with notes, upon which she'd written: *Libro. Puerta. Ventana. Refrigerador.* Some days, when I returned home from school, I found her stretched out on the sofa, a wet washcloth pressed to her eyes, repeating after Elena and Raul as they ordered drinks at a bar or searched for a museum. At dinner, she said things like, "Pass the *mantequilla, por favor.*" When Father joked that Elena and Raul must have been saving the verbs for later, mother scowled and said, "*Muy* funny."

Some time before the Mexicans arrived, Mother invited Nonna to lunch. "Very fancy," Nonna said, as she unfolded a linen napkin and set it on her lap.

"It's just a napkin," Mother sighed. "Now let's talk about Ray."

Nonna tasted the soup, declaring it better than last night.

"You weren't here last night," Mother said.

"You said it's leftovers. Soup is always better the next day."

"We were talking about Ray," Mother snapped.

Nonna nodded and asked for the pepper. While she peppered her soup, Mother complained that Ray would ruin everything. "He'll boast about his car or some other of his possessions."

Ray had an Edsel. It was splendid! It was pale orange with a creamy roof and reminded me of a Dreamsicle. Soon enough, the Edsel would become a laughing stock, a symbol of corporate ineptitude. But these were the first heady days of production and Ray was riding the crest of the craze's wave. He was first with everything. Polaroid camera. Color TV. Aunt Vivian had a baby blue Princess phone on her nightstand and their kids had hula-hoops before anyone else.

"Nobody wants to hear about Ray's car," Mother said, and reminded Nonna that the Mexicans had a silver room and a Diego Rivera.

"It's a nice car," Nonna said. "Later, you'll give me the recipe for the soup."

Mother, provoked by Nonna's evasions, said, "Vivian never should have married Ray." Then she called him a *bulvon,* and I wondered if that was the same as when Grandfather called Ray, "A bull in China's closet."

I already knew the story of how Nonna and Grandfather pushed Vivian into marrying Ray Sugarman. Mother told me the story the way some mothers read *Pippi Longstocking* to their daughters. "Your Nonna and Grandfather had an arranged marriage, so don't talk to those two about love," she'd said. "They actually believe you could learn to love, especially someone who squires you around town in a fancy car, wines and dines you at Fritzel's and the Blackhawk, and proposes to you at The Cape Cod Room."

Ray's mother, Eloise Sugarman, was the icing on the cake. Eloise lived in a residential hotel on The Gold Coast. "Chestnut Street. A good address," Mother would say, in a preening imitation of Nonna. The fact that Eloise had been set up in the hotel by her shady brother, Hymie Weiss, never entered into Nonna's calculations. It was no secret that Hymie made his money jackrolling drunks outside a South Shore saloon owned by a petty mobster named Willie McNab.

"Those two turned a blind eye to all that," Mother told me. "They were dazzled by the restaurants, the fancy address, the car."

But Eloise didn't have enough to keep her son in pocket money for Fritzel's for the rest of his life. So Ray Sugarman became a bill collector, complete with an alias. Joe Beam. That enthralled me. Joe Beam! Father insisted Ray was a bill collector only because he wasn't smart enough to follow in his uncle's footsteps.

Mother dredged all this up at lunch and when she finally wound down the only sound was the clattering of Nonna's spoon as she nervously scraped her bowl. Finally, Mother, her hazel eyes flashing, said, "Well?"

Nonna, avoiding Mother's gaze, dabbed at the corners of her mouth with the napkin, careful not to leave lipstick stains. "Well what?"

"Aren't you going to say something?"

"What do you want I should say?"

"Anything!" Mother exploded.

"Ray will behave," Nonna softly rejoined.

"How do you know?"

"*Oy*, please. Leave me alone. I didn't make the world. I'll speak to Pa. He'll take care of it."

"What's Pa going to do?" But before Nonna could reply, Mother suggested place cards, which she probably had in mind all along. Her plan was to corner Ray. Nonna would be seated to his left, Mother to his right, and Father directly across from him.

"Place cards." Nonna nodded solemnly. "Very fancy."

❖ ❖ ❖

The troika—Father's name for Nonna, Vivian and Mother—squabbled over everything, including who would host the first dinner for the Mexicans. Since Paul was her brother, they eventually conceded the honor to Nonna. Next they argued over Vivian's suggestion that everyone be at Nonna's before the Mexicans arrived. "Then what?" Mother groaned. "I suppose you want us to hide in the kitchen and jump out when they arrive and yell, "*Sorpresa!*" Mother wanted people to gather at Nonna's as usual, which meant everyone would be late, though some would be later than others. "We don't want to appear too eager," she said. She was big on scripted nonchalance.

The menu took days to resolve, though not out of concern for the particular belief or immune system of any given guest. Back then, guests politely ate what was served. Nevertheless, Aunt Vivian questioned whether the plum compote that Nonna served at the end of every meal was suitable for the occasion. "My *pflaumen* is good enough for the Queen," Nonna sniffed. When Mother offered to bake a marble cake to accompany the fruit compote, they all calmed down.

Nobody in our family drank, except ceremonially at Seders and the Sabbath. But Mother, who'd attended the lively parties hosted by her aunt and uncle at restaurants in the Zona Rosa, wanted wine with dinner. When she demonstrated the way Paul signaled for another bottle by motioning to the waiter with an arched eyebrow and a slight nod to his empty glass, Aunt Vivian snorted, "'When in Rome,' is what I say. They'll just have to get through a meal without wine." When Mother peevishly suggested that Ray pick up a case of beer from the South Side saloon where his Uncle Hymie had rolled the drunks, Vivian leaped to her feet and started clearing the lunch plates. Nonna unfastened the top button of her blouse, fanned her face with her hand, and said, "Somebody get my ice bag." In the end, they agreed they knew nothing of wine and delegated the task to Father.

And in the end, Nonna agreed to remove the plastic covering from the sofa, but not without a fight, which was waged by phone in one of the troika's endless round robins of calls. "It's got to go!" Mother shouted, so I knew she was talking to Nonna, though I didn't know what she was talking about until she said, "Because they'll stick to it in the heat. And it's ugly!" Then mother phoned Aunt Vivian to report that Nonna had just hung up on her. "You've got to talk some sense into her. They have a Diego Rivera."

The troika had a phone system that was so elaborate Father joked smoke signals would be easier. It had begun after Aunt Vivian moved to the suburbs, where she could make unlimited phone calls, even back to the city, without an extra charge. But the reverse was not true; Nonna and Mother had to pay a "long distance" fee for every call they made from Chicago to Skokie. If Nonna wanted to speak to Aunt Vivian, she dialed Vivian, quickly hung up after one ring, and waited for Vivian to return the call from her toll-free aerie. Mother signaled with two rings.

Their system ended abruptly during the peak of the protective plastic crisis, when Ray happened to pick up the phone in the middle of the first ring. "Stop!" Vivian screamed. As she grabbed the receiver out of his hand, he lost his balance and hit his head on the kitchen counter. Instead of rushing to his aid, Vivian called Nonna back to apologize for Ray's transgression. Over lunch at our house, Mother and Nonna clucked sympathetically when Vivian reported that Ray had accused her of setting a bad example for the kids. Then Mother suggested putting the system on hold "until this whole thing blows over."

❈ ❈ ❈

After Nonna phoned to say she'd buy the flowers herself, Mother called Vivian and said, "Go with Ma, or we'll end up with carnations. Please." Vivian was having a migraine and told Mother she would have to go, but Mother was baking the marble cake for the big dinner.

Since Nonna didn't drive, and I was five years away from a driver's permit, and Nonna refused to let Grandfather drive because he would pace the sidewalk outside the flower shop and make her nervous, we took the bus to Hlavacek's.

Mrs. Hlavacek led us to a cooler near the back of the shop. "This will be perfect," she said, pointing to an elaborate arrangement behind frosty glass doors. *Perfect for what?* I was about to say, since we hadn't yet told her what we wanted. Later, I learned that Mother had phoned ahead and instructed Mrs. Hlavacek to make an arrangement for seven dollars, a lot of money then. But before I could speak,

Nonna said, "Very nice." I thought so, too. There wasn't a single carnation in the bunch. But there was the most amazing flower I'd ever
seen—a Bird of Paradise. Its orange petals sprouted like plumage
from a tall stalk that jutted obliquely to form a beak. It looked like it
might take flight at any moment. "Very nice," Nonna repeated, and a
beaming Mrs. Hlavacek marched the flowers to the front of the shop
where she set them on the counter and lovingly swaddled them in
layers of pink and purple paper. She finished off the package with a
flourish of ribbon and held it out to Nonna, as if presenting her with
a gift. Then she handed Nonna the bill, and Nonna, who must have
forgotten that she had to pay, had a dizzy spell.

The doctor called Nonna's dizzy spells, "revenge of the nerves."
Mother called them *fake*. "Sarah Bernhardt has nothing on your
grandmother," she'd say. But Nonna wasn't acting. Her face grew
flushed, beads of perspiration broke out on her upper lip, and she
started jabbering in Yiddish, which she resorted to whenever she
became flustered. At home, she would have unbuttoned the top two
buttons of her blouse and fanned herself with whatever was handy,
while someone ran for the ice pack. In public, she stayed buttoned
up and pressed a rose-scented handkerchief to her nose.

Remembering the flower cooler, I led Nonna to the back of the
store and pressed her forehead to the refrigerated glass, while Mrs.
Hlavacek, who'd been muttering gibberish and flapping her skinny
arms like a grounded bird, allowed the distance between us to grow,
as if she feared dizziness was contagious.

When we finally made our way back to the front of the shop,
I told Nonna that she could pay with the fifty-dollar bill she kept
tucked in her brassiere. She replied with another dizzy spell, this

time swooning and pitching forward. Luckily, she was petite, a tiny wren, so I easily broke her fall and managed to get her seated on the floor. Her back was pressed against the counter and her legs stuck straight out in front of her like a doll I once had whose stiff plastic legs hinged only at the hip. Nonna's skirt was hiked up to her knees and one of her sandals had come loose. The flowers lay limply in her lap. The ribbon had fallen off the pretty papers, which by then were rumpled. Emerging from the wreckage was the bird's head, its plumage so bedraggled it appeared to be molting.

Nonna frowned at the tattered wrapping, then glanced at me, glanced at the door, glanced back at me, smiled sheepishly and shrugged.

"We have to pay for them," I whispered, though Mrs. Hlavacek was at the back of the store with a man who had come in asking for roses.

With a fingertip, she prodded the bird's head until it wobbled from the end of the strong stalk. "It's broken," she said.

"We still have to pay for them," I said, struggling to keep the irritation from my voice.

"I don't have money," Nonna said.

"You have the fifty," I hissed. It was the same fifty-dollar bill Nonna had been walking around with for as long as anyone could remember. She wouldn't even break it the time she was looking after us and I needed money for a school field trip. Because of Nonna, I spent a day with the third graders while all the fourth-grade kids went to the Shedd Aquarium.

"It's in there," I said, pointing an accusing finger at Nonna's breast.

She pushed my hand away and in a tone I'd never heard before, said, "What's the matter with you?"

Stung by her anger, I shouted, not caring what Mrs. Hlavacek heard. "What's the matter with *you?*" I was scared. I'd never witnessed Nonna fall apart in public. "The money is in your bra. You've got to use it. The Mexicans are coming." I started to cry.

"Oy, please, Sophie," Nonna said, fanning herself with her hand. "You don't understand."

"Then tell me," I said, wiping my eyes with the back of my hand.

"You're too young. Some day, you'll understand."

"Are we making any progress?" Mrs. Hlavacek chirped, trying to sound friendly and polite in front of the man buying all those roses.

"We're fine, Mrs. Hlavacek! Nonna's standing on her own two feet now," I said, as I hoisted my grandmother off the floor. To Nonna, I said, "Let's pay for these and get out of here. Mother's going to be looking for us."

Nonna gazed lovingly at the flowers in her arms, as if she were cradling a newborn. Gently, she set the bundle on the counter and without a word took my hand and dragged me to the front of the shop. Years later, I can still hear the bell jingling as the door closed behind us.

❋　❋　❋

Drinks before dinner were served on the three-season porch, which was separated from the dining room by a sliding glass door. Nonna reserved its lone piece of furniture—a bamboo love seat with jungle-print cushions—for the guests of honor. Everyone else gathered around on the metal folding chairs Grandfather had dragged up from the basement that morning.

The Indian summer heat hadn't let up, but Nonna, always at war with dust, refused to open the jalousie windows more than an inch.

A noisy ceiling fan clicked like a metronome, though nobody in the ragged circle kept time to its beat.

Nonna and Uncle Paul sat huddled together, bantering in Yiddish. They laughed like schoolchildren, swapping stories in the language they had shared before their world turned upside down and they scattered to a new one. Nonna had on pretty green shoes and pale pink pearls that matched the buttons on her blouse. Despite the heat, Uncle Paul wore a tie and a starched white shirt with silver cufflinks. He was a deliberate man, imbued with Old World charm and elegance. Mother said Paul spoke so many languages he could start a sentence in one and finish it in another. Not even my princely father possessed such quiet assurance, and certainly Ray, who arrived wearing Bermuda shorts and black socks with tennis shoes, did not.

Father and Ray were thrown together like the last two kids in gym class waiting to be picked for a team. Father sat smiling through thin, pressed lips. Mother called it his "social smile." Ray, who did all the talking, must have been going on about his car.

Aunt Vivian kept jumping up to check on dinner, making her way to the kitchen in small, syncopated steps, humming the "Banana Boat Song" under her breath. She had on something peculiarly floral, reminding me of the gathered skirts we had to make in Home Ec, though she bought all her clothes at Marshall Field's.

Grandfather, who wasn't much for small talk, kept running out to the yard, yelling at the kids to slow down before somebody lost an eye.

Mother and Shelita sat locked in a conversation that involved much hand gesturing and facial expression. Mother was dressed like she was ready to dance a fandango, or like Ava Gardner in *The Barefoot Contessa*, only she was wearing strappy sandals. She had on a white peasant blouse that draped loosely on her shoulders, and a narrow cotton skirt cinched with a red sash. She'd flung a red shawl over the back of her chair.

Shelita, in pale blue shantung silk, could have been going to tea with the Queen. Her ring fingers sparkled with precious stones. I'd heard Mother say Shelita had so many rings she grew an extra finger to accommodate them all, but I only counted five on each manicured hand.

Shelita spoke with her eyes, bright one minute, dark and hooded the next. They darted around the room like fireflies, alert to everything. Except for her animated eyes, she was a study in stillness, so composed she might have been balancing a book on her head. Very possibly one nestled among the folds of her raven hair, which was piled high like an elaborate bird's nest.

"Sputnik! Schmutnik!" Uncle Ray's voice erupted through the din. He leaped to his feet, his face purple, his neck veins bulging. "Do you think for one minute the Russkies could launch a satellite into space? That thing's a hoax. A fakenik."

The room went still. Even the ceiling fan appeared to go quiet. Mother should have told Ray to pipe down. *Sit! Sietete!* Or Grandfather should have sent him home to change out of his plaid shorts. Father might have done something other than gaze down at his glass. Uncle Paul adjusted his cuff links. Nonna unfastened a nacreous button and pressed a sweating glass to her forehead. Shelita's eyes darted so wildly I thought they might follow Sputnik into orbit.

The lilting sounds of "Day-O" drifted in from the kitchen, drawing closer as Aunt Vivian playfully shimmied back to the porch. "Day-O," she crooned. "Day-ay-ay . . ." She froze. Her smile collapsed.

Her shoulders sagged. One side of her ornately upswept hair escaped its pins. She said, "Did somebody die?"

"Oy, please. Such talk," Nonna said, dabbing at the top of her lip with a scented handkerchief.

Aunt Vivian shot Ray a baleful look and he dropped back into his chair. Then she turned to Father. He had been sitting as nobly as the Duke of Edinburgh, but sounded like an errant schoolboy when he said, "I merely pointed out that we're wasting our engineering talents on the wrong things." He frowned at his melting ice cubes. "We should be launching satellites instead of rolling out flashy cars with all that razzmatazz. Now they have Sputnik." He paused. "And we have Edsel."

"It's people like you . . ." Ray shot to his feet again, pointing an accusing finger at Father. "People. People who . . ." he blustered. "You sit there smug, thinking you have all the answers."

"Barry heard Sputnik on his ham radio," Mother chimed in. She was patting Shelita's hand, as if her aunt was the family dog afraid of thunder. "He said the beeps are in the key of A-flat."

"Barry?" Ray snorted. "Suddenly, your son's an expert. How does he know what a satellite sounds like?"

Mother started to speak, then stopped. How *did* anyone know what Sputnik sounded like?

If only she hadn't faltered, for Ray seized the moment and barreled ahead. "I figured the kids were monkeying with the remote," he said. "Then I read that garage doors were picking up signals from Sputnik. Going up and down, just like that." He snapped his fingers, the star sapphire on his pinky catching the light as he demonstrated the speed with which his garage door had spontaneously

56

opened and closed. "God damn Russkies." He grinned, shaking his head in mock disbelief, then turned to Uncle Paul. "Say! Do you have garages down there?"

Paul was short and wiry, but had the presence of a much larger man. He appeared at ease with himself. "Please, explain," he said, his clear grey eyes dancing. "How does a fake satellite open a door?"

Ray dismissed Paul with a wave of his flashy hand. "The Mexicans couldn't launch a tamale," he chuckled.

Nobody spoke. Mother continued patting her aunt's hand. Father's smile was so tight I feared he'd been afflicted with a palsy. Nonna appeared about to undo another pearly button and Uncle Paul fixed his steady gaze on dark, thickset Ray.

Perhaps everyone figured that Ray would run out of juice, like a battery that keeps its charge until suddenly it doesn't. But Ray was jazzed. He asked Uncle Paul what kind of car he drove, only by now he was calling him Pablo.

Before Paul could reply, Ray started in on his Edsel. "I decided on the pale orange model with a cream-colored roof. The white-wall tires are a bitch to keep clean, but are they ever gorgeous." He rubbed his fingers together, suggesting such features don't come cheap.

"I made a killing on the market," Ray boasted, perhaps to distinguish himself from his felonious uncle, the one who rolled drunks outside the saloon. "Made up for the big hit I took after Lou gave everyone that hot tip." He winked at Grandfather. "Right, Lou?"

Mother dropped Shelita's hand as if she'd exhausted her powers of consolation. Father drained the melting ice from his glass. Nonna fanned her face with the handkerchief. Nobody ever brought up Cuprex. "What's done is done," Nonna had instructed the family. And then Ray blurted the story to Shelita and Paul. They had a Diego Rivera. A silver room. A maid to pour coffee. They did not need to know that everyone in the family, upon grandfather's advice, had bought shares in a failing South African copper mining company. "That's the last time I'll take any advice from him," Ray bellowed.

If there are depths to silence, the room grew profoundly still. Even Shelita's eyes stopped darting, though Nonna and Mother gave each other "the look," which means they locked eyes, thinking nobody else had observed the knowing glance that passed between them. Then Mother leaned forward, began speaking to her aunt, but stopped. Not even in English could she explain what had just transpired.

Grandfather broke the silence. He rose, removed his spectacles, wiped them with his handkerchief, and with his gentle brown gaze exposed, said, "You need broken eggs to make an omelet." Then he slipped the glasses back on and sat down. Heads nodded. A sense of relief passed through the room, as if a soft breeze had slipped through the cracks of the jalousie windows.

Only Ray looked askance at Grandfather. "How long have you been in this country, Lou?" He paused and the only sound was the hypnotic clicking of the fan. With a chuckle, he said, "The expression is, '*You've got to crack a few eggs . . .*'"

"Oh, shut up Ray." Aunt Vivian sprang to her feet, the other side of her hairdo coming undone. I wanted her to start singing again, to shimmy and light up the room. Instead, she looked like a reveler at the tail end of a long evening, instead of the niece of a Royal Couple who had come for dinner that hadn't yet been served.

Ray blustered on. "You've got to crack a few eggs," he repeated, pausing between each word so that even Shelita might have understood. "To. Make. An. Omelet." Finished, he sank back in his chair with a satisfied grin.

Nobody ever corrected Grandfather. That rule was more inviolable than the one about never to reveal family secrets. Besides, we were all so accustomed to his mixed-up sayings that we barely noticed when he said things like, "You can't make lemons from lemonade," or, "The papers in the U.S. make from a fly such a big thing." They were as much a part of him as his rimless spectacles and stingy brim fedoras—white straw in summer, dove grey felt in winter.

❊   ❊   ❊

Dinner was served. That's all I want to say about that. We never did sit on Nonna's sofa after dinner. We didn't even go outside to look up in the night sky for Sputnik or chase fireflies in the dark.

The place cards, of course, had been beside the point. By the time dinner rolled around nobody said much of anything, not even Ray, whose batteries had finally run down. Cutlery clinked. Dishes were passed. Compliments were paid. During the lulls, the faint clicking of the ceiling fan in the other room could be heard. Grandfather, who was forever lecturing that we don't own shares in the electric company, had forgotten to turn it off. This was one of those occasions where a dog would have come in handy. Barry tried livening things up with a joke about a sandwich walking into a bar. Mother threw back her head and laughed, though she'd heard it before. Shelita politely flashed a confused smile. Others tittered with relief. Then everyone got back down to the business of eating.

Occasionally, Nonna would say, "The brisket's too dry." In unison, everyone, even Ray, protested, "It's perfect!"

The strangest part of the meal was the severed head of the Bird of Paradise floating in a crystal bowl in the center of the table. Mother had gone back for it and the rest of the flowers, after she pulled the marble cake from the oven.

The Mexicans stayed the week and, being good sports, made the rounds of all the family dinners. During the days, Shelita shopped, with Mother along as interpreter and guide. Perhaps that explains how Shelita ended up buying a dozen silk camisoles at Marshall Field's—two in every color. Mother, who still hadn't moved on to verbs, refused to consider that anything got lost in translation. Instead, she blamed the excess on her aunt's immoderation, which she said was par for the course. "A dozen. You'd think she was buying bagels."

Years later, I visited Mexico City. Paul, by then, had scattered to his final resting place. Shelita was an old woman living in a luxury high rise on the edge of Chapultepec Park. One of her sons, the one who had the tantrum when his snowballs melted, arranged a visit, calling ahead, as if I'd requested an audience with the Queen. "Mother needs time to put on her lipstick," he explained.

When I arrived, Shelita was seated in a brocade wing chair with a mohair throw covering her lap. She smiled up at me through plum-colored lips. Above her was the Diego Rivera. There it was, the portrait of Shelita. She was looking out at something that must have caught her eye.

Buona Sera

"**I**'M HOME!" LYDIA CALLS OUT.

"*Dov'è la biblioteca?*" says Lyle, though not in greeting. He's at the stove, his back to her, tossing something into a pot. His voice is steady, reassuring, as seductive as the all-night jazz radio host who inhabits the parallel universe that of late has revealed itself to Lydia—a world populated with graveyard shift workers, or people like her, who have lost the innate ability to sleep.

"*Dov'è la biblioteca?*" he repeats, and this time Lydia sees the wires dangling from her husband's ears, as if he were plugged into himself. Lyle, the multi-tasker, is practicing Italian while he cooks. Lydia is supposed to practice, too, but she resents the cheerful prattling of Flavia and her boyfriend, Gianni, who hold tedious conversations with Florentine waiters, museum guards and shop clerks. Now one of them appears to be in search of a library.

Lydia places a bag of Chinese takeout on the counter before swooping in to hug Lyle. She comes up from behind, burrowing her face into his wooly sweater, which smells faintly of onion and sandalwood soap. He sets down a wooden spoon, plucks the mini-speakers from his ears letting them drape around his neck, then turns to greet her. *"Buon giorno, signora!"* He smiles and pecks her cheek. "Or is it *sera*?"

Lyle, a high school English teacher, is one of the last sticklers for syntax and grammar. He teaches his students to parse sentences; he corrects their spelling, though the current orthodoxy dictates that such nit picking stifles creativity. Lydia has tried assuring him that it will not matter if he wishes people a good evening before the appointed hour. What she hasn't said is that she may not go, that she's not ready, as he put it when he surprised her with the tickets to Rome, to "move on."

"What's in the pot?" she asks, her voice too bright. She's banking reserves of goodwill before confessing that she's already seen to dinner, that on her way home from seeing Dr. Becker she stopped at Wing Yee's. "Chili," he says. As if to dispel any doubt, he tosses a handful of minced jalapeño into the cast iron pot.

"Smells good," she says, wrinkling her nose with feigned delight. "Who's the author?" Lydia doesn't feel up to playing this game, but she's still hoping to atone for the dinner mix-up. Every school year, Lyle takes on a new project, and this year has been no exception. What started as a joke, after he'd read an essay, "How to Cook a Wolf," turned into his Moveable Feast project. Lyle will lure his students into the world of books through the pairing of readings with recipes. So far, he has prepared Mrs. Cratchit's holiday pudding, and a vegetable noodle soup suggested by a passage in *Middlemarch* that details the annoying manner in which Mr. Casaubon scrapes his bowl with a spoon.

The other day, Lyle showed Lydia a recipe for Jim Harrison's mesquite-roasted doves, which began: *Find some wild doves. Shoot them.* When they finally stopped laughing, they stood frozen, embarrassed by their mirth, which had seized them without warning. What to do with such unexpected—and yes, unwelcome—pleasure? Lydia had been about to apologize, when Lyle pulled her close and kissed the top of her head, delivering them both from the discomfiting spell.

"Simon Ortiz," Lyle replies, holding the spoon to Lydia's mouth. She recoils, then with a rueful glance toward the Chinese takeout, accepts his offering, though she has little enthusiasm for food. It's all the same to her, which is the reason she couldn't understand why Lyle had stormed out of the house last week when she snatched the marmalade from his hand. After safely setting the jar back on the windowsill beside the others, she retrieved some strawberry preserves, but by the time she set it on the table Lyle had left the room, and soon she heard the front door click shut.

He issued his ultimatum later, after he returned home, sweat-drenched from a run. "It's me or the jars, Lydia," he said, packing the floor as he spoke, head bowed, hands clasped behind his back, as if he were measuring the length of the room with his feet. He had on orange running shoes, the color of popsicles. She'd been about to ask if they were new, when he said, "A year is enough."

When she asked if he'd actually leave because of some jam jars, he looked at her and with a grim little smile, said, "You know it's not that."

She remembers looking up from the orange shoes to the jars, like amber frozen in time, perched on the sill above the sink. "He's right, Lydia," they seemed to say. "A year is enough."

Then she heard herself say—to the jars or to Lyle, she still can't be sure—"The man in the truck would understand."

Lyle stopped pacing. "What man?"

She told him then about the man who drives around with a coffin in the back of his pickup. When Lyle looked even more puzzled, she explained. "His son was killed while on patrol in Najaf?" She spoke in that annoying interrogative lilt, that verbal tic that afflicts so many young people, turning every declarative sentence into a question. It was as if she couldn't bring herself to assert what she knew was true.

She told Lyle that the coffin holds a few of the son's belongings: a soccer ball, a pair of his favorite shoes, his boots, uniform, dog tags. The side panels of the father's truck are plastered with poster-sized photos: the son in uniform; the son blowing out the candles on a birthday cake, a paper hat askew on his mop of dark curls. "He, you know, the man, was in all the papers. On the radio," she'd continued, again with that annoying, hesitant inflection. She'd heard him on a radio call in show.

She didn't tell Lyle that she'd picked up the phone to tell the man that when her husband isn't home she sets Phoebe's picture on the windowsill beside the jars. But another caller came on the air and accused the man of dishonoring his son's memory, so she hung up and turned the radio off.

When Lydia said, "Surely, you've heard of him," Lyle shrugged and shook his head and she hated him for his indifference. She couldn't get the man's voice out of her head. "My son's off to Iraq. And there I was at home learning that there's no weapons of mass destruction," he said, nervously letting out a puff of laughter. He was soft spoken, his speech lightly accented, the way she imagined Gianni might sound if he spoke English. "I had two TVs going all day long, and the radio, trying to get news, to figure out what is happening over there. I see sandstorms, the Tigris River, tanks. I see Marines move through dark alleyways. They kick in doors. All the time, I am afraid for my son, but I am helpless."

Now Lyle is pressing a spoonful of the literary chili to Lydia's mouth. Despite everything, he still needs her approval. She opens wide, feigning delight at his offering. "Mmm. Do I detect a hint of cinnamon?"

"Nice touch, isn't it?" He beams.

She offers to set the table, and when he says the chili won't be done for at least another hour, she says, again, too brightly, "That's all right. We can have it tomorrow." With a nod toward the paper bag, she confesses that she's already seen to dinner.

He turns abruptly and the glasses, which he has recently started to wear for reading, slip, so it appears that he's peering down his nose at her. She braces for a fight, but his voice is as soothing as her favorite radio host when he says, "I told you I was cooking." But she can tell by the slope of his shoulders, by the way his tall frame has collapsed in on itself, that he is too tired to argue.

Lyle returns to the chili and while Lydia sets out two dinner plates, she considers what, if anything, she can say to atone for the mix up. The truth is, she passed by Wing Yee's on her way home from Dr. Becker's, and bringing dinner in had seemed like a good idea at the time.

Lydia, who has no desire to share her innermost thoughts with a stranger, is seeing Dr. Becker at Lyle's insistence. This afternoon, she told Dr. Becker: "Lyle wants the marmalade gone. That's why I'm here." She didn't tell her how on sunny days the light filters through the jars, creating an incandescent glow. And she could never say, as the man in the truck did: "My world tumbled, and I felt my heart go down to my feet and rush back up through my throat." She couldn't even say, "Save me." Instead, she described Lyle pacing, measuring the room with orange feet while issuing his ultimatum.

Phoebe had found the marmalade recipe in a dog-eared *Sunset* in the orthodontist's waiting room. It was sandwiched between recipes for persimmon pudding and fig pie—desserts conceived for people with backyard trees yielding bumper crops. Their yard in Minneapolis, in a growing zone unable to sustain such exotics, yields nothing more than acorns. Lydia remembers thinking they'd have to buy the oranges, as well as the kettle and jars and tongs. Turning to Phoebe, she'd said, "It's a lot of work." But when Phoebe flashed a tinsel grin and said, "It will be fun," Lydia believed her. Besides, once she got hold of an idea, there was no stopping Phoebe. Nothing. Nobody. Not Lydia. Not Lyle. Not Lydia's mother, who threatened a hunger strike if Phoebe didn't come to her senses. But that was later.

So they made marmalade as if they had their very own orange tree out back, instead of an old oak that shed a prodigious amount of inedible nuts. They danced to Paul Simon while they scrubbed and chopped, boiled and stirred.

Now Lyle, who has been chopping green pepper, looks up from the cutting board, and in a voice suddenly tight with anger, accuses her of forgetting. "How could you?"

"I just did," she says. Hoping to leave it at that she starts fussing with the alignment of the tarnished forks and spoons. Her mother had given the set to her after selling the house. Lydia had protested that it was too much, too soon. "Besides, what will I do with silver?" When Ida replied, "Some day you'll pass it on to Phoebe," Lydia had relaxed. The gift felt like insurance, a guarantee of a logical progression, that everything happens in turn. Some day it would be Phoebe's. Now the dulled utensils feel like a rebuke, a symbol of Lydia's failure to oversee and protect the natural order of things.

She picks up one of the dulled spoons, rubs it with the hem of her silk blouse, holds it up for inspection. Though the job clearly requires more than elbow grease, she continues buffing, as if she can erase the dull miasma, which, like acid rain or nuclear fallout, cloaks everything around her.

She sets the dulled spoon down and looks at Lyle, who's gone back to his chili. Now would be the time to find a way to cut through the anger and resentment choking the room. She has always derived immense satisfaction from the sort of quotidian exchanges that pertain to the upkeep of a home, that signify a shared existence—reminders about the plumbing, car repair, dry cleaning. It's possible that over time such minutiae, and particularly the need to discuss them, might wear a couple down, but she has always found the exchange of such ordinary—some might say mind numbing—detail, to be extraordinarily intimate. Who else besides Lyle needs to know, or for that matter, even cares, that the car needs a new muffler, or the leak in the living ceiling is coming from the bathroom on the opposite side of the house, or his shirts won't be ready until Friday?

Now, though, as soon as she says, "The tree is coming down first thing tomorrow," she senses her blunder. This can only remind Lyle that she'd cancelled the previous appointment, which had taken six weeks to procure, as well as the one before that.

He nods, which Lydia reads as permission to press on. "What's 'first thing,'" she says, straining for a light-hearted tone. "Is it seven o'clock? Maybe eight!" She pauses. "Though perhaps eight o'clock is second thing."

Once, this might have gotten a rise out of Lyle-the-Stickler, but as he tosses more diced pepper into the pot, he accuses her of trying to change the subject. His voice is eerily composed, as if he has just asked her to please pass the butter. Then he says, "I told you I was cooking dinner. How could you forget?" "It seemed like a good idea." She waits a moment, then says, "At the time, I mean. I was driving past Wing Yees and it seemed like a good idea at the time."

She crosses the room to where she'd set the bag, carries it to the table, flops down in front of one of the places she'd just set, unfolds the bag that Mr. Yee's daughter had sealed with the swift, assured precision of an origami artist, pulls out a carton, picks up one of the tarnished spoons, and plunges it right into the heart of General Tso's chicken. "Lydia!" Lyle rushes toward her, still clutching the knife, hair falling over one eye, ear buds flapping, the Italian lesson pouring out of them. Briefly, she wonders if he plans to use the knife on her, though Lyle has always been the gentlest of men.

He stands over her, pleading with her to stop. But she shoves the spoon into her mouth knowing that she can't stop. She eats a mouthful, licks the spoon clean, then plunges it back into the carton for more.

"Lydia, please! For God's sake, stop. Please. Stop." The very words that he (she, too) should have said to Phoebe.

When she digs in for another helping, he yanks the spoon from her hand sending a gob of chicken, red-hot chili peppers and congealed sauce sailing across the room, where it hits the window, oozes down the glass pane, and lands on one of the amber jars.

Quickly, he grabs a towel and starts mopping the mess that landed in Lydia's lap, but she pushes him away and rushes to rescue the sullied jar. It nearly slips from her trembling hands as she tries to wipe it clean. She is too shaken up to speak, but if she could she might suggest that he see the shrink. Let him, the one who flew into a rage over a carton of Chinese chicken, sit in a cramped office in an overstuffed chair, confronted by a box of man-sized tissues, a vase of leggy carnations, Dr. Reena Becker's long, crossed legs extending down to a pair of three-hundred-dollar stiletto heels. Everything about that place is calculated to make Lydia feel small.

But she's tired. Lyle is, too. She can see that now. Even the tan he has acquired from all that running can't mask his pallor. She wonders if the strain in his face is a new development, or something else she's neglected to see, like the tarnish, or the tree, which has been dying in stages? "Oak wilt," the forester had said. And then, as if it were any consolation: "It's wiped out half the trees in the city."

Lydia resists the urge to cross the room and stroke her husband's check, push his hair back, press close to his sandalwood aura. She remembers the night before the funeral, the way they'd comforted each other with their bodies. The clinging had felt so familiar that it was hard to believe that everything else in their life wasn't also the same. It was their subsequent couplings that felt indecent, a betrayal of something, their better selves, perhaps.

She sets the jar back on the sill and says, "I'm sorry."

That's what she'd said to the men who stood on her front porch, in their dress greens, their pant creases sharp as if Mr. Yee's daughter had pressed them. The pink-cheeked man wasn't much older than Phoebe. At first Lydia wondered if he might be one of her daughter's old boyfriends. Then he called her "ma'am," and she wanted him to be one of those clean-cut proselytizers who sweep through the neighborhood now and then—a Mormon or a Jehovah's Witness.

Through the screen door, the older man, identical to the first in nearly every way, except for the color of his skin, asked to come in.

"I'm sorry," she said. "I'm sorry, but you can't come in."

She was in a hurry to get back to the kitchen, where she'd been preparing marmalade as a surprise for Phoebe, who was due home in sixteen days. It was a lot of work, as she'd predicted all those years ago, though it had never felt arduous when the two of them worked together. But without Phoebe, even Paul Simon sounded flat, so she'd turned the recording off. That's when she heard the sound. It was the lightest tap on the door that she'd ever heard.

"Ma'am, we need to come in," the young man insisted. He was fresh faced, barely shaving.

"I'm sorry, but you can't."

Then his partner asked to speak with Lyle, with "Mr. Martin."

When Lydia said, "He isn't home," they offered to wait.

Lydia, who ordinarily supplied the men who work on her house with pitchers of lemonade in summer, mugs of hot coffee when it's cold, closed the door, retreated to the kitchen and turned the recording back on to drown out the sound of the knocking. Then she wiped the cooling jars, and moved them to the sill, thinking back to a time when she and Phoebe had stood admiring their handiwork, pleased as if they'd just lifted delicate raku bowls from a kiln.

It was Lyle, still flush from his run, who let the men in. How could he know? He wasn't like her, consumed by fear as she finished those jams without Phoebe, fear that even gentle-sweet Paul Simon couldn't assuage, fear set off by knowing, knowing, absolutely knowing why those men in starched greens were standing on her porch. How could Lyle, punch drunk on endorphins, know? So he let them in.

Later, Lyle told her how she'd run to the piano for the picture of the three of them, then waved it in their faces, pointing to Phoebe, who was being swung in the air by Lydia and Lyle, one moist, dimpled hand tucked inside each of theirs. "You're wrong!" she'd shrieked. "Mistakes happen!" Hadn't they heard of death-row prisoners? DNA? "You've come to the wrong house!"

Then she ran back for the picture of Phoebe swinging a tennis racket, vintage Phoebe with the crooked smile and the perfect teeth.

"My daughter is nineteen years old," Lydia cried. "She was captain of the high school tennis team." She jabbed a finger into the starched chest of one man and then the other. "Was it you? Or was it you?" she cried. "Which one of you came to campus and promised to teach her to fly?"

When Phoebe had phoned home to announce her plans, Lydia said: "Tell them you didn't mean it." Then she hung up and scrubbed the kitchen floor and ironed all the laundry, including Lyle's boxer shorts and socks. Lyle, who had never done so before, put on a pair of old gym shoes and ran around the block three times. Lydia's mother, Ida, called Phoebe and said, "If it's flying lessons you wanted, why didn't you tell me?"

Then Lydia called Phoebe back and reminded her of the picture on her grandmother's living room mantel, the one taken minutes before Ida and her first husband, Harold, who was on a weekend pass, were married at City Hall. The newlyweds spent their brief honeymoon at the old Edgewater Beach Hotel, where Harold carried Ida over the threshold, into a room filled with orchids. As a child, Lydia never tired of listening to her mother tell that story, though she wished it didn't have to end with Harold stepping on a land mine. She used to fantasize that, had he lived, Harold, King of the Romantics, would have been her father. Even after she was old enough to understand that, had he lived, she never would have been born, Lydia wanted the story to have a different ending.

Phoebe was killed by an improvised explosive device. "An IED, ma'am," said the baby-faced man.

"IED?"

"Sharp metal objects," said his partner.

Back and forth they went.

"Remote detonators."

"Garage door opener."

"Doorbell."

"Easy to make."

Together: "Nobody's sure just how it went off."

Lydia can't shake the idea that IED is one letter off from IUD, the contraceptive device that had failed and given them Phoebe. She's never been able to share that particular thought with Lyle, who, after adjusting the burner to simmer, informs her that he's going out for a run.

When she's sure Lyle's gone, Lydia retrieves the picture, the one she's kept hidden in the pantry since the day Lyle the grammarian, the stickler for the precise turn of phrase, railed against her "fucking shrine." When she tried explaining, when she told him about the pot-bellied Buddha and the plate of mandarin oranges and incense arranged on the floor near the cash register at Wing Yee's, he rolled his eyes and she slipped the picture into a drawer.

Now she sets it on the sill beside the jars. There's Phoebe, in a straw hat and goofy sunglasses, laughing as Lydia and Lyle swing her off the ground. Lydia and Lyle are laughing, too. Lydia can't recall shoving the photo in the officers' faces, though she remembers that after they left she beat Lyle on the chest with her fists; she punched his stomach. She screamed. "You let them in!" Later, after all their friends had departed, leaving them alone with a refrigerator full of plastic-shrouded casseroles and cakes, she told Lyle, "I opened the door and when I saw the men in dress greens I knew. I knew. But I thought that as long as I didn't let them in, they couldn't tell me. And then it—none of it would have happened. But then you let them in."

Lydia is suddenly aware of voices and panics at the thought that Lyle may be right, that she really is crazy and it has come to this—auditory hallucinations. Then she sees the Ipod, which he'd left on the table. She tries turning it off, gives up, and instead plugs the mini speakers into her ears. Flavia and Gianni are in a *trattoria*, where Flavia is dithering over whether to order *carne* or *pesce*. Lydia has had enough of Flavia and her unexamined life. She's had enough of Flavia, to whom nothing untoward happens, unless you count the time her luggage was lost at the airport in Prague, where she and Gianni had gone on holiday. She didn't care whether Flavia recovered her lost bags and she certainly doesn't care whether Flavia orders meat or fish. She yanks out the ear buds and sets the rambling device back on the table.

Their own dinner is in shambles. Chili á la Simon Ortiz? Or General Tso's chicken? The chili is simmering, but she sees that the offending take-out carton, as well as the rest of the order, is gone. Perhaps Lyle tossed it out when he left the house, though more likely he would have set the remains in the refrigerator. She hopes it's the latter and is about to check when a shadow crosses the room. Looking up, she sees a squirrel perched on the window ledge, gnawing on an acorn. They've blanketed the lawn this year, and she remembers the arborist explaining that it happens, that a dying tree can still produce acorns, even an abundant crop.

Tomorrow the tree comes down. Earlier, when she'd reminded Lyle of that, she'd wanted to thank him for his patience and understanding. Last month, when she confessed to canceling the tree cutter, she'd jokingly called it, "A stay of execution." But then she started to weep about the impending loss, and he said they could plant another. When she bristled at the suggestion, he admitted that a new tree wouldn't be the same. Then she stopped whimpering and shared with him the first thing that came to mind: "We can try planting an orange tree." He might have said, "You're fucking nuts," or more likely for Lyle, "You *have* gone round the bend, haven't you?" Instead, he went for a run.

She loves that oak tree. It has served them well, gracing the yard with a canopy of leaves, providing shade on the sultriest of days. It has provided fodder for squirrels; a blaze of color every fall. Dormant, it stood silhouetted against the sky, a majestic reminder of seasons to come. Like the silver her mother had passed down, it stood as insurance against the vagaries of life, a symbol of consistency and order.

Lydia resists the notion that death is an inevitable part of that order. Phoebe didn't have to die. Not in that desert. Not in that trumped up war. Not, she thinks, ever. No. That's not true. The truth is: Phoebe didn't have to die now. Not in that way. Not while Lyle was running through the streets in his day-glo shoes and she was sorting laundry.

She taps on the window now and calls out, "Enjoy it while you can!" The squirrel drops the nut, leaps off the sill and as it scurries toward the safety of the tree, Lydia grabs Lyle's plaid shirt off a hook near the back door and heads outside where she begins to rake the acorns. They resist the pull of the rake, yet she manages to gather them in small piles, her arms burning from the effort. Her hamstrings throb as she bends to scoop them up. Tomorrow she will feel the effects of all this effort, but now she feels a brisk surge of energy, the kind that causes lights to blaze before shorting out in a storm. Suddenly, she knows how Lyles feels when he runs—exuberantly exhausted.

As she scoops the last of the acorns into the bag, she wonders if a bumper crop portends a harsh winter—record snowfall, ice storms, extreme cold? At that, she turns the bag over and calls to the squirrel. But night has fallen, and if it's still out here, she can't tell.

Heading back toward the house, she sees a light goes on in the kitchen. Lyle is back from his run. She ducks behind the tree and watches as he opens the refrigerator. Perhaps he'll take out the Chinese, stand over the sink and eat it straight from the carton, as she's caught him doing in the middle of the night, when he can't sleep, either. Instead, he stands with the door ajar, swigging orange juice from the carton. There was a time when she would have reminded him to close the door, drink from a glass, and he wouldn't have objected.

After closing the door, he looks around as if he's suddenly forgotten the reason he came into the room. Under her breath she reminds him to check the chili and he does. As he starts toward the stove she knows they haven't lost that eerie telepathic power that some close couples possess. He stirs the pot, brings the spoon to his mouth, but stops short, sets the spoon down and heads toward the window.

Lydia feels a catch in her breath, not because she's afraid he can see her (he can't see out into the dark), but because he is reaching for one of the jars. He wipes it with the hem of his t-shirt, carries it to the table and sits before one of the places she'd set. He taps the lid with one of the tarnished spoons, and she wants to cry out to him to stop. She can run back to the house, but she'll never reach him in time. All she can do is hide behind a diseased tree and spy on her husband, waiting for him to break the seal, which may be the very thing that is holding her together.

As she watches him wrap his hand around the lid, she feels light-headed. She closes her eyes and leans into the tree, until the dizziness passes. By the time she opens her eyes, the lid is off and he is dipping a spoon into the jar. He takes another spoon and then another, but she doesn't falter. Even after he scrapes the jar clean, she remains steady on her feet. "That leaves four," she whispers, knowing, just as she knows the tree is coming down in the morning, that at breakfast tomorrow she'll open another jar and spread marmalade on a triangle of toast. She will give a jar to the mailman and perhaps one to the man who comes to cut down the tree, which she ducks behind again, just as Lyle goes to the window and scans the yard, as if he knows she is out there.

"Buona sera!" she calls out. "Or is it *notte*?"

She knows he can't hear her, yet he seems to shrug, as if to say that such distinctions arc unimportant. Then he turns, and the last she sees of him, his hands are clasped behind his back, his head slightly bowed, as if were taking a measure of the room.

I Bet You Didn't Know

EVERY SATURDAY, THE YEAR SHE TURNED TEN, MOLLY AND HER mother rode the train into the city where she spent the morning learning to make art. Her teacher, a large-boned woman with perfect posture and pinned-up hair, toured the galleries with her students, before turning them loose in the classroom to paint. The teacher was fond of religious art, particularly portraits of Mary. *The Annunciation. Madonna con Bambino. Mother and Child.* She instructed her students to paint Mary.

Molly painted her great grandmother instead. She painted Rose holding a wooden match to a pair of silver candlesticks as she ushered in the Sabbath. Molly had only seen her great grandmother in a single photo, taken when Rose was a young woman strolling arm in arm with her husband down Vienna's Ringstrasse. Molly's mother would look at that photo and say, "Corinne has my grandmother's candlesticks. They should have been mine."

So Molly painted candlesticks. And she painted candlelight reflecting off Rose's face, rendering her as beatific as all those Marys on the museum walls. She painted Rose with a nimbus of hair, soft as the clouds upon which putti and angels sit as they hover over the Queen of Heaven. Molly's teacher said, "You didn't follow instructions." Molly's mother said, "Very nice. But that's not my grandmother, and those are not her candlesticks."

"Golly, Miss Molly," Jonah said, when she told him the story. "I kind of like your mother. I wish you hadn't told me that."

"You can go on liking her. I just thought you ought to know." Six months later they were married.

Now Jonah is saying, "Peruvians were eating popcorn before they were using pottery."

"Oh, lah di dah! You with your ribbons of information." Molly slumps back in the car seat and sighs as he challenges her to come up with something better.

Neither one of them can recall the first time they played *I Bet You Didn't Know*. Molly insists they invented the game along a deserted stretch of highway in Montana, somewhere between Fort Benton and Roundup. Jonah agrees the dearth of cars would have had a chilling effect on license plate bingo, but he swore a long drive through west Texas put the kibosh on that. (Jonah uses words like *dearth* and *kibosh*. That is one thing Molly loves about him. Or is it two?) Once, when she said, "Texas. Montana. They're all the same, really," he swerved to the side of the road, cut the engine and reached for his Rand McNally. "Here's Texas," he said, then dragged his finger to the top of the page and showed her Montana.

She loves him for that, too, for his insistence on the truth. Jonah is a fact checker for a hallowed weekly magazine. Precision is his métier. If he were a watch, he'd be a Breitling, a Rolex. He'd be Greenwich Mean Time. Yet he hasn't always stuck to the truth. Shortly after they'd met, he told Molly that during his junior year in college he ran away to Spain and fell in love with a barebacked horse rider in a circus. "But she had nothing on you," he said. Now he has lobbed the first volley in their game, with the bit about Peruvians and popcorn. And she can't think of a thing to top it.

"I'm waiting," he says, turning to her with a wide grin.

She shrieks at him to keep his eyes on the road. He's a terrible driver, looking at her when he speaks, darting in and out of lanes without signaling. Lately, they have been in the car a lot, driving to a hospital or a funeral or some other place they'd rather not be. "Driving toward misery," she calls it. This evening they are heading out to see her mother.

Jolene phoned this afternoon. "You'd better come see," she'd said. When Molly pressed for more, Jolene replied, "She'd be better off chasing fireflies with a thimble." When Molly asked Jonah what that meant, he said, "Beats me."

Now she asks if her mother might have something like post-traumatic stress.

"That's highly unlikely," he says. "It's not as if she was in a crowd when a bomb went off."

"I suppose you're right," she sighs, slumping deeper into her seat. "I just wondered if being in the news again might have triggered something. That's all."

"It's *not* PTSD," he asserts, and launches into a lecture on the syndrome. Molly, who has only to look at Jonah to feel the bluebird of happiness fluttering in her chest, tells him to shut the fuck up.

❊ ❊ ❊

She steps cautiously along the flagstone path to the back door. Jonah trails behind, carrying the wicker basket filled with her mother's favorite foods—lentil loaf, Belgian endive with avocado, a sourdough baguette. Gingery ginger snaps from the bakery near his office.

Molly plans to set the dining room table with her mother's favorite plates, the ones with the pattern of apricots, peaches and plums. "The stone fruit dishes," Charlotte calls them. Molly and Jonah have invented an elaborate story in which the fruit gets high.

She rings the bell and is about to ring again when Jonah sighs and says, "Just use the key."

The kitchen, to her relief, is bright as starched linen. It smells faintly of vinegar and soap. An abundant spray of purple dahlias graces the breakfast nook table. Had she only imagined Jolene's summons?

Though Molly is certain her mother has heard them, she cries out, "We're here!" which is how Jonah enters his family home. There, Carlo will bound into the room and leap on them with sloppy paws. Jonah's mother, Lizbeth, will call from wherever she is, "I'm here, too!" Now they are greeted by one of her mother's silences.

She finds her mother in the study, tossing books into a box. Volumes that once ranged the shelves are strewn across the floor, piled on tables, tossed onto chairs. Adding to the confusion, a jumble of pots and pans is scattered about, as if the kitchen had taken leave of its senses and migrated to this wood-paneled refuge in the back of the house. Her mother is standing amid the clutter like an elegant, long-legged bird. She has on loose-fitting silk pants; her delicate blouse is a drift of pink.

"Knock, knock." Molly approaches as she would an unfamiliar dog. She thinks of Jonah's mother, rushing to embrace her, singing, "Molly! Molly!"

"Sit down," Charlotte says, rather wearily. "You're making me nervous standing there like that."

Molly flops onto a velvet loveseat, one of the few surfaces not besieged by books.

A silence settles over the room as Charlotte continues tossing books into a box, her gossamer sleeves flapping like butterflies with every motion.

Molly grasps that Jolene had not adequately prepared her for this. Briefly, she considers all the ways she might ask her mother: *What are you doing?* Then, yielding to inertia, she closes her eyes and wishes for a dog to come bounding into the room, a dog like Carlo, who, in his exuberance, is forever knocking things over in the Hartman household. Or perhaps she should wish for something more dramatic. A violent thunderstorm. A tsunami. Anything to rattle this old house, from the rafters on down. This is the effect her mother has upon her. She has Molly wishing for a natural disturbance. Or a dog. But her mother loathes house pets. And there will be no tsunami to inundate this richly appointed home in the landlocked Midwest.

When she opens her eyes, she sees a spray of blue anemones in a white vase. "The flowers are lovely," she says.

"Jolene bought them."

"Jolene?"

"Jolene is perfectly capable of buying the flowers herself."

Molly does not doubt Jolene's competence, but this particular arrangement is lifted straight from a painting. For years, her mother has imitated the tableaus created by Matisse. Today, in her flowing garments, she resembles one of the artist's odalisques. "Well, they're nice," she offers.

"I've often wondered," Charlotte says. "All that fuss over Mrs. Dalloway and the flowers." She holds up a book, as if it were the very one under discussion, then casually tosses it into a carton. "I mean, who else would buy them?"

Molly gazes at the flowers, wondering whether she should remind her mother that, after all, *she* had entrusted someone else—Jolene—to buy them. Or she might say that she loves Clarissa Dalloway's determination, her resolve, her delight in a mission, even one that pertains to something frivolous as flowers. What courage it takes to step out into the world, innocent of how a seemingly ordinary day can unfold.

Seeing no other way, Molly retreats from the safety of flowers and plunges headlong into the matter at hand. But then she is tripped up by the annoying verbal tic that turns the simplest assertion into a statement riddled with doubt. "It looks like you're moving?"

"Let's just say I'm moving things along," Charlotte says, casually tossing another book into a box.

Funny that. After *the incident,* which is what Molly and Jonah have taken to calling her mother's fall, Molly moved back home for a few days, though Charlotte had injured nothing more than her stubborn pride. At home again, that time, Molly was struck by how little had changed—or been moved along—in the twenty years since she'd departed for college. She camped out in her old bedroom reading Nancy Drew and listening to records she hadn't heard since high school. Quickly, though, the comfort she'd found in the familiar surroundings was replaced by a disquieting sense that she was not unlike an inhabitant in a museum diorama, one depicting the life of a long lost tribe, perhaps one that ate popcorn from bowls fashioned out of gourds.

During what she came to regard as her days in a time warp, Molly hovered in the wings, emerging now and then with pots of tea or small plates of food, beseeching her mother to eat. "It's your favorite," she'd say. "An English muffin with marmalade." Then she remembered Charlotte's favorite ginger snaps. "Look, Mommy! See what I brought." Yes, thirty-eight years old and she'd reverted to *Mommy*. This, she reasoned, was less a regression than an awkward attempt at instilling in her mother a sense of purpose. If nothing else, Charlotte had a role to fulfill as mother to a child, albeit one who was fully fledged.

After a few days playing nursemaid, Molly announced her departure.

"Where are you going?" Charlotte had asked.

"Back."

"Back where?"

To my life, Molly should have said, though lamely she replied, "Back to Jonah. Back to work. They need me at the office."

"What is it that you do?" her mother said, vaguely.

Molly designed catalogues for a women's athletic clothing company. She loved her work. "Stop being perverse," she snapped. "You know what I do."

Charlotte gave a graceful shudder. "All those art lessons. All those Saturday mornings into the city so you could finger paint."

In fact, Molly had taken classes in brush stroke and composition. She experimented with watercolor. Charlotte roamed the galleries while Molly "finger painted."

"Oh, Mommy," Molly said. "I have to go. Besides, I live across town. It's not like I'm going anywhere. And you have to pick yourself up. Get out. Do something. "

Rather touchily, Charlotte had said, "What's out there that I don't have in here?" and Molly wondered whether the answer might be lurking beneath the mohair throws or crushed velvet cushions. Patterned rugs blanketed the wide-planked floors. Paintings covered the walls. Even Charlotte's French teacher came to the house for her weekly lesson. Later, when Molly told Jonah that she honestly could not say what was out there that her mother did not already possess, he said, "The silver candlesticks?"

Now Molly considers the jumble of books. The pots. Pans. She recalls the concern in Jolene's voice. *Just come.* "If this is about the painting . . . ." Her voice trails off.

"Sometimes, Molly, you can be so tiresome," Charlotte says, then reaches for a saucepan.

Molly remembers her mother returning home with pots and pans she'd scrounged at tag sales and second-hand shops. The cookware multiplied. "She referred to the pots as *the disappeared*," Molly once told Jonah. "You make them sound like victims of political repression. In Argentina, to be precise," he'd said. "But your mother's family wasn't from Argentina." To which she replied, "True. But their belongings were confiscated. They disappeared. She wanted them back." When Jonah said, "It's doubtful the pots and pans your mother bought were part of the plunder," Molly gave him the stink

86

eye and said, "Sometimes, Jonah, you can be annoyingly rational."

Now, Molly crosses the room and begins rummaging through a carton.

"Get out of there," her mother says, rather sharply.

But Molly continues digging through the box, finally emerging with a book. "You can't be serious," she says, holding it up for her mother to see. "The family album? You're getting rid of family pictures?" She wants to say, *During fire season in southern California, people set their photo albums near the front door. They're the first thing people save. After the dog. I bet you didn't know!*

"I mean it, Molly. Put that back," Charlotte says, as if Molly was five years old and had just tossed a bag of potato chips into the shopping cart.

Molly cradles the album, as if it were a cat she'd brought in from the rain. Charlotte's grandmother Rose is said to have stuffed it into her suitcase when she fled, along with the candlesticks, which she'd wrapped in a flannel nightgown. After Rose died, the album and the candlesticks went to Charlotte's mother Sadie. For years, the album stayed on the coffee table in Sadie's living room, a room reserved for special occasions, which, as far as Molly knew, never arrived. *Not today,* Grandma Sadie would say, whenever Molly asked to see the pictures.

Again, Charlotte admonishes Molly to put it back. Molly shakes her head and backs up. Charlotte follows. When Molly is backed into a corner, Charlotte holds out her hand and demands the album. "No!" Molly shouts. She feels defiant, the child who trespassed into Grandma Sadie's living room one afternoon and was punished for her transgression. Charlotte tries prying the album out of her arms, but Molly clings to it. Breathlessly, she pleads with her mother to stop. But Charlotte's grip is firm. She is surprisingly strong. And then, as abruptly as it had begun, their tug of war is over. The album goes sailing through the air and photos rain down like confetti onto the Persian rug.

Molly drops to the floor, her hands shaking as she tries to gather up the grainy images. She anticipates a rebuke, but instead is admonished with punishing silence. For a brief moment all she can think is that she will need hinges. She wonders who, if anyone, still sells such things. And she wonders how she will put the pictures back in order. Then she begins to cry for the inhabitants of the album, whose world, so meticulously resurrected in these pages, had come unhinged.

She pauses at a photo of a young girl on a garden bench. The girl appears to be posing for a portrait. In one corner, in the shadows, an artist sits with a sketchpad on his knee. The girl is wearing sandals and a frock with a ruffled hem. A brindled tabby lies curled up in her lap. When finished, the portrait will be known as *Pearl with Cat.*

The photo of Pearl is one of the many "before" pictures in the album, one taken *over there* when life was still right side up. *Over there* was across the ocean. Pearl had disappeared *over there.* The cat, too, Molly supposed.

Molly was six, about the same age as the girl with the cat, when she asked, "Where is Pearl?" In time, she learned that Pearl was a cousin of Charlotte's grandmother Rose. Pearl had an older sister, Channa. In one of the photos, Channa is seated in an outdoor café, looking down at a book. She is wearing a beret; a string of pearls. There is no photo of Channa at a camp near Auschwitz, where she was forced to sort the plunder from Jewish households and pack it into barrels. There is no photo of Channa coming across her parents' wedding photo or of the armed guard who stood over her as she removed it from its silver frame. Years later, Channa revealed that she nearly fainted as she tossed her parents' picture into a pile for burning. The frame went into a barrel with all the others.

With a different mother, Molly might have grown up like Jonah, listening to *The Wind in the Willows*. Instead, she was weaned on stories like the one of Channa, forced at gunpoint to destroy her legacy. Molly's mother would look through the album with her, pointing to pictures, saying, "She went to the camps. He did, too." Molly had tried to imagine the person in the picture going to a place like the one in Wisconsin where her brother went every summer, returning home with lanyards, potholders, and mosquito bites painted pink with calamine lotion. Even when Molly was old enough to know better, she couldn't imagine the people who populated the album doing anything other than what they were doing the moment the shutter clicked—posing stiffly in front of mountain lodges; sitting quietly in cafes; or smiling out at the world from beneath striped beach umbrellas. She tried to imagine these people filing naked toward the "showers," making their way past armed guards and attack dogs, only she could never see beyond all the paraphernalia of a life in progress—high heels, fur-trimmed coats, linen suits, straw hats, sunglasses, sandals. She couldn't imagine Pearl or any of the others being rounded up, then sorted and selected for death, discarded as easily as the peaches Jolene described as "too far gone for summer pie."

Once, after closing the album, Charlotte had said, "You know, Molly, the dish did not run away with the spoon. That sort of thing happens only in nursery rhymes. Over there, the dishes and spoons could not escape. Neither could the forks, the pots and pans. Everything went into barrels. This is how you destroy all traces of a people. In a barrel, a pot is just another object. It sits doing nothing; being nothing. Useless. Inutile. Do you understand?" She'd paused before trilling, "*Superflu*," the French oddly softening the blow.

Too young to understand, Molly had said, "But where is Pearl?" Charlotte sighed, "Oh, Molly. If life were a nursery rhyme, we'd all be happier." For the first time, Molly wondered: *Are we not happy?*

Now as Molly picks herself up off the floor, Charlotte says, "They're going, Molly. I've made up my mind. The pictures must go."

Molly reminds her mother that Channa was forced to discard her parents' photo. "Besides, who would want our family's old snapshots? Paintings, yes," she says, thinking of *Pearl with Cat*, which has never been found.

"Oh, Molly, Molly. Have I taught you nothing? They even took light bulbs." Reaching for a pot, she says, "When I bought this, I imagined a time when . . . Oh, never mind." Gently, she sets the pot in a box. "I thought I could rescue the past by holding onto things." The room falls still. Then she says, "Everyone in that album is dead. Gone. Nothing will bring them back. Now go dry your tears."

❊ ❊ ❊

Jonah was at a meditation retreat when it happened. Upon his return, he said, "Tell me everything I missed."

The world might have imploded while he sat on his tuffet. Even the food they served at the ashram, the gastronomic equivalent of a hair shirt, brought to mind curds and whey. What had he missed?

90

Another school shooting? Congressional gridlock? Freaky weather? Beheadings! "*Nada*," Molly replied. "Well, actually." And after some hesitation, she told him.

"What painting? Where? How?" Jonah erupted with questions.

As he stood before her in baggy drawstring pants, dun-colored sandals and heavy wool socks, she marveled at how quickly love can turn to something she could only describe as its flip side. Crossly, she replied, "What difference does it make?" But then, recalling how her love for Jonah had always flipped right side up again, she said, "The point is, newspapers on this side of the ocean and that had a field day with the story. Now the world over, the woman I first knew as *Mommy* is known as *The Clumsy Art Lover.* She's the woman who tripped, lost her balance, and fell into a painting, ripping the canvas and cutting its value in half."

"Poor Charlotte," Jonah said. And when he cooed, "Poor Molly," her heart flipped back to where it belonged. And when he asked, "How did it happen?" she confessed: "I asked the very same thing."

"I fell. That's what happened," Charlotte had said, when Molly came to fetch her. She was seated in a wheelchair, a guard standing over her, as if she were being discharged from a hospital and not a major metropolitan museum of art. "They must have feared I'd fall into a few more on my way out," Charlotte groused, as she launched herself out of the wheelchair and marched briskly beside Molly to the car.

At home, Molly served tea, which Charlotte sniffed, then rejected. "I don't like chamomile," she said.

"It was in your cupboard."

"It must be Jolene's."

91

"It's soothing," Molly said, urging her to try it.

"It tastes like boiled weeds. Besides, I don't need soothing. I'm fine."

I'm not, Molly thought, remembering the meeting she'd been called away from, then the long drive from the museum, her mother in the passenger seat, nose pressed to the window, refusing to speak. She lifted her cup. "Chin chin!" she chirped, then grimaced and set it down. It *did* taste like weeds. "Now tell me what happened."

"Suddenly, everyone was swarming around me, shouting at once. 'Look! It's ripped.' 'Oh, my God!' 'What a klutz.' 'How could she do that?'" Charlotte gazed unhappily into her cup. "How could *I* do that? That's rich. Where were all those art lovers during the plunder? But they only wanted to berate *me.*" Lifting her gaze, her eyes steady on Molly, she said, "You know that what I did was nothing compared to what *they* did."

"The people in the museum?" Molly said. "What did *they* do?"

"I'm talking about them," Charlotte said, impatiently. "The ones who took what was not theirs. The ones who stole our legacy." She rose and left the room, returning with a bulging folder, from which she handed Molly a neatly clipped news article. After reading about a man in Munich who'd lived for years among more than a thousand paintings stolen by the Nazis, Molly looked up at her mother and said, "But what does any of this have to do with today? With the painting?" She tripped over her words. "Today's picture." She paused. "It wasn't ours."

"What wasn't ours is ours," said Charlotte, inscrutable as Jonah's Zen master. She reminded Molly that *Pearl with Cat* has never been found. She spoke vaguely about crimes against humanity. "So it *is* ours," she said, her voice trailing off. "In some way." Then, frowning at her untouched tea, she plucked a sugar cube from the bowl. "My grandfather sucked his tea through sugar cubes," she said. "When the sugar dissolved on his tongue he'd smile and say, 'Life is sweet.' I remember how the mood in the room shifted. The air felt lighter, the Sabbath candles burned brighter. Then Grandma Rose would glare at him. 'What is sweet?' she'd say. 'Tell me.' Once, when he held up a sugar cube, she said, 'For horses, maybe. But for people? Oh, Lou, Lou, Lou. You think you can make everything better with a lump of sugar?' I'll never forget what he said. 'Please, Rosie. Leave me be. Give me this moment of sweetness.'" Charlotte glanced down at her chamomile tea, then, fixing her gaze on Molly, said, "I hated Grandma Rose for infecting the house with her sour moods. It took years before I understood that she couldn't allow herself the simplest pleasures. Not even a lump of sugar. She got out in time. She was afraid to ask for more."

Molly had looked broodingly at her mother, who, even in distress, appeared meticulously elegant. How like her to hijack the conversation, which in this case would require, on Molly's part, some consoling remark, even an approving nod. Undeterred by her mother's theatrics, and yes, even unmoved, she steered the conversation back to the present. "This painting you ripped." She stopped and started as she felt her determination slipping away. After a long silence, she said, "Do you know that it was stolen?"

"That's not the point."

"I thought that *was* the point. *Your* point, in any event."

"Never mind," Charlotte said, with a dismissive wave of her hand. "It's a minor work in the artist's oeuvre. And they'll fix it. By the time they're through, it will look better than new. Nobody will suspect a thing. What I did is a trifle in the damages department. A piffle."

❋ ❋ ❋

Charlotte is quietly pushing bits of lentil loaf from one side of her plate to the other, while Jonah natters on about a solar storm heading toward Earth. The sun, it appears, is expected to spit out giant bursts of radiation. "Coronal mass ejections," he says. "But don't worry. These flare-ups won't affect the weather. Only radio communications. The Earth's magnetic field. GPS. Things like that."

Molly has little understanding of what *things like that* (how unlike Jonah to lack specificity!) do. She finds it worrisome that such *things* might suddenly become immobilized, like plastic windup toys—chattering teeth, monkeys on motorbikes—that skitter about, until they do not. Without such *things*, perhaps the world will go into a tailspin, fall off course, flip upside down.

She is about to ask him to elaborate, when Charlotte, suddenly animated, looks up from her plate and says, "Honestly, Jonah. The things you know." She volunteers that Mme. Pefley had canceled their French lesson the other day because her daughter had run away from home. "Perhaps these sunbursts affected her daughter."

Molly assumes her mother is joking, so when Jonah says, "I wouldn't know," she wants to scream. *Go out on a limb, Jonah! It won't kill you to say, "Anything's possible, Charlotte."* But speculation is anathema to fact checkers.

"Well, whatever the cause, her daughter ran away and Mme. Pefley was too distraught for our lesson," Charlotte says, sounding bemused, as if distress under such circumstances was as improbable as a solar ejection affecting the weather.

Jonah, always on more solid ground sticking to matters of fact than to the messy tangle of emotion that, say, a runaway daughter might engender, says, "I've been meaning to tell you, Charlotte. You were right. The painting is good as new." After repeating the news they'd all seen in the morning paper, that the painting is back on display, he suggests an outing to the museum.

Charlotte inclines her head to one side, as if the gravity of Jonah's suggestion has brought it down. Her face is pale in the candlelight. Her limpid blue eyes appear to be looking off in the distance. She seems not fully present. Yet her voice is strong. "Let the curiosity seekers check it out," she says, reprovingly. "They'll flock to see it—a minor work by a major artist. Let them find some flaw, some breach in the canvas that's beyond repair."

"But they say the picture's good as new," Jonah insists.

"Someone also said that canvas has a memory," she reminds him. "How did he put it?" She pauses. "Ah, yes! 'Once ripped, canvas has a tendency to return to the distortion caused by the accident.'" Gazing unhappily down at her plate, she says, "I'm surprised you didn't catch that, Jonah. They had to gently coax the fabric back to its original state." She tugs lightly at the hem of her weightless sleeve, as if it, too, might be persuaded to lie flat. "When I read that," she continues, "I wondered if people have a similar tendency? Do we keep returning to some distorted state? We're born in a state of grace, but once we fall, do we keep on falling? They sent me packing in a wheelchair, after all. Afraid I'd tip over and ruin another treasure. But really, I'm not the enemy. They should focus on the looters." Then, rather obliquely, she says, "But who am I to assign blame? I don't even have my grandmother's candlesticks."

Molly holds her breath, praying the moment will pass, but before she can exhale, Charlotte is telling Jonah, "My brother stole them, you know."

SUBTLE VARIATIONS AND OTHER STORIES

Jonah nods, as if he hadn't heard this before. "He took them while my mother was in the hospital," she continues. "He couldn't even wait for her to die."

Molly glares at Jonah, signaling him to end the conversation, but he looks right through her and leans in toward Charlotte, who is saying, "He gave them to . . ."

"Stop!" Molly clasps her hands to her ears. "I can't listen to this. I'm tired of the candlesticks."

"Molly," Jonah says, rather sharply. "We were just talking."

"That's not just talk," she corrects him. Then, turning to her mother, she says, "You wouldn't use them, even if you had them."

"Candlesticks go to the daughter," Charlotte says, with calm authority, as if stating some immutable law—gravity or entropy.

"Is that a fact?" Molly asks Jonah. "Perhaps there's a source, something that spells out the rules for bequeathing candlesticks, like the protocol for ascension to the throne or the presidential order of succession." She pauses, looks from Jonah to her mother, then back at him. "Oh, it doesn't matter. She only wants Corinne—the *shiksa*—not to have them."

"Corinne wouldn't use them," Charlotte snaps.

"No. *You* wouldn't use them. You'd tuck them away among all your other bibelots. They would tarnish, if not for Jolene, who *would* use them. For her voodoo. For her God. Or gods. Oh, stuff!" She props her elbows on the table and cradles her face in her hands.

"Get your elbows off the table," Charlotte says. "And stop talking nonsense."

"Corinne had to study with the rabbi, learn all the blessings. Bone up on ten thousand years of Jewish history," Molly says, folding her hands in her lap. "She went to the mikvah before the wedding. She would bless the candles."

"It wasn't a mikvah. It was Vivian Sugarman's swimming pool."

"It was a standing body of water."

"Your palavering is giving me a headache," Charlotte says, and picks up her fork.

"She would use the candlesticks," Molly says. "That's all I'm saying."

"She'd be playacting."

"At what?"

"At being a Jewess."

"Why would she do that?"

"Beats me." Charlotte sets down her fork. "Perhaps the rabbi omitted the chapter on pogroms and massacres. Failed to inform her that everyone hates the Jews. Didn't mention the wells we were said to have poisoned. The matzo seasoned with the blood of Christian children."

Molly sends Jonah a beseeching look, but he is preoccupied with a piece of bread and a butter knife. She looks out the window. It has begun to drizzle. Raindrops are streaking the glass. They could talk about the weather. Isn't that what weather is for? Instead, she says, rather abruptly, "At least the candlesticks didn't end up in a barrel."

It is Charlotte who mentions the rain. Then she picks up her fork and begins to eat.

❋ ❋ ❋

"If I were to run away, would she be distraught?" Molly asks. They are in the car, heading home.

"What's that, Miss Molly?"

97

"My mother. Would she be distraught, if I ran away?"

"You're too old to run away," he says, with the confidence of a fact checker.

She flops her head back against the seat and says, "Oh, Jonah. Am I really?"

"Yes, my love. Far too old."

"In that case, perhaps I shall die," she says, dramatically. "I suppose I'm old enough for that."

"But if you are dead, you'll never know how your mother would have reacted. Besides, then *I'd* be distraught."

Now would be the time to lean over, brush a hand against his cheek, kiss him. She wonders if he knows that she might have married him, even if she hadn't loved him. Her need to be part of a family that appeared not to have a care in the world was that strong. She loved Lizbeth, who smelled like rising bread dough and put toothpaste on her husband's toothbrush in the morning to move him along. She even loved the family dogs. Yes, she could inch closer to Jonah and kiss his cheek. But she feels immobilized by all this talk of death and distress. What they need—though she is too tired, even for that—is a cheery round of *I Bet You Didn't Know.*

After a long silence, she says, "If this story were to begin, 'Once upon a time,' where would it start?"

"The silver candlesticks?"

"Oh, the candlesticks," she groans, sinking deeper into her seat. She doesn't want to talk about them, especially not with Jonah. She thinks of his mother's indifference to things. The first time Jonah brought her home, Molly swept a ceramic vase off a table while demonstrating Jackson Pollock's splatter painting technique. When she dropped to the floor to gather the shards, Lizbeth was beside her, murmuring, "Oh, Sweet Potato, stop your crying. It's just a thing."

"That sounds like Lizbeth. Old hippie dippie Lizbeth Hartman," Charlotte had said upon hearing the story. Molly regretted telling her mother that Lizbeth had lived on a commune for a few years after college, baking bread and tending the chickens and bees. Had she really expected her mother to be charmed by Lizbeth's lack of concern for the vase, her indifference to things?

Yet Lizbeth's family's belongings hadn't been seized. Nor, for that matter, had her family members. Lizbeth Hartman, *nee* Williams, can trace her ancestors back to the earliest settlers. "Not counting Native Americans," Jonah told Molly, soon after they met. "So they were what? Pilgrims or something?" she'd asked. Later, she learned that Lizbeth once drove across country to visit the graves of family members she'd discovered through census data, ancient ship manifests and family-tree chat rooms. Soon after Molly and Jonah were engaged, Lizbeth sat her down and showed her photos of the grave markers, as if she were introducing Molly to all the relatives who'd sent their regrets, sorry they could not attend the engagement party.

Molly had stared at Lizbeth's pictures in quiet disbelief, and thought of her own mother pointing to pictures in *her* family album, saying, "She went to the camps. He did, too."

Now she looks over at Jonah, gripping the steering wheel, staring intently at the road. Dear, sweet Jonah. He should have married that circus girl in Spain. She reaches over, gently brushes a fingertip to his cheek and whispers, "I've got one."

He nods.

"My great Aunt Lillian invented fitted sheets."

"Fitted sheets?" Laughing, he slaps the steering wheel. "That's not an invention."

"Fitted sheets are nothing to sniff at," she snaps. "Try sleeping without them. See if you aren't all tangled up in the bedding by morning."

"Still, I'd hardly call that an invention," he says, and asks why she'd never mentioned an Aunt Lillian.

"She died when I was young," Molly replies, though she doesn't offer that Lillian went mad after the death of an infant daughter. *A blue baby*, people had whispered. For a while Molly painted pictures of blue babies and called it her Blue Period. Sometimes, she painted blue numbers onto the arms of the babies, like the numbers tattooed onto the soft underside of her great Aunt Channa's arm, the woman who once read a book in a café and later was forced to toss her parents' wedding picture into the burn pile.

Molly inches back to her side of the car seat, thinking she should concede the game. Then she leans over and slips a hand into the wicker basket at her feet, feeling around until she finds it. It's there. The photo of Pearl and her tabby. Later she will paint their portrait.

She sits back in her seat and stares ahead. The rain has stopped. "There's the moon!" she says. She considers saying, *When I was young, while you were nestled in your mother's lap listening to* Wind in the Willows, *my mother told me that the dish did not run away with the spoon. I bet you didn't know that.* Instead, she says: "So the cow jumped over the moon."

Playfully, Jonah says, "And the dish ran away with spoon."

"We all know that," she sighs and looks wistfully at her husband faithfully steering them home. "But where did they go?"

100

Summer Is for People

LEV RETURNS FROM THE PARK EAGER FOR BREAKFAST. HE PULLS his chair across the tired linoleum and calls out, "Won't you join me? Your show can wait." He hates the way he sounds, like a grown man coaxing a cat from a tree.

The kitchen table—the kitchen being an extension of the room where Galena occupies the sofa—is set with the same breakfast she's been laying out for over fifty years: thick slices of rye bread; sweet cream butter; stewed figs and prunes; a boiled egg balanced in a porcelain cup. A napkin is threaded through a pewter ring. Only Galena is missing. She is no longer at the table with the newspaper or a shopping list, awaiting his return from the park. She no longer fixes her hair before breakfast or colors her lips. This morning she is still in her robe, and now, as he begs her to join him, she dismisses him with a flick of her hand.

Lev considers telling Galena about the empty bottle. Usually, the bottles are so small a child couldn't get drunk. Worse is the mouthwash. "They'll drink anything," he once explained to her, an archeologist spinning theories to make sense of other worlds. It wasn't so long ago when he would return for breakfast and report such findings, as if he'd been on a treasure hunt, and not a personal mission to clean up the space others litter with abandon.

As he taps the eggshell with the back of a spoon, Lev considers all the turns their conversation might take. *Last night, our friend got lucky.* After a pause, he might say, *Well, maybe not so lucky. The vodka. It was Polish.* Flirtatiously, she'd flick that dismissive hand, as if to say, *You, with your jokes.* He and Galena could communicate like that, with a hand gesture, a shrug, a raised eyebrow. But this silence is different. He misses her.

She used to challenge his assumptions. *Our friend,* she might snort. *How can you be so sure there's only one who drinks and sleeps in the park?* He imagines her shaking her head in disbelief, even disapproval. Possibly both. *Homeless. Here. In America.* She'd sigh. *What were we thinking?*

She can pull him under just like that, with her moods. In no time, she will have him believing that it is normal to sit in a dimly lit room staring at the television or blasting music from a tinny cassette player. She'll wear that contraption out with her Jan Peerce singing *Fiddler on the Roof.* She loves all the songs. Her favorite, *Anatevka,* she blasts while cooking dinner or dusting the chifforobe. The great tenor's voice floods the apartment, masking Galena's silences. If Lev moves to turn down the volume, she holds up a hand, tears streaming down her face.

In the park, everything is different. There, even on the bleakest days, he feels lighter, buoyant, filled with a sense of possibility. Just the other day he heard himself exclaim, "Summer is for people!"

They were all gathered around the picnic table. The sisters, Sonia and Rachel. Solomon Polachek, who'd been laid up for a month with shingles. Larissa, whose husband dropped dead of an aneurism last spring, just like that. Yet she carries on. Morris Reznick and his wife Natalia. Not even Morris, who picks a fight over every little thing, had blunted Lev's delight over summer. Nobody gave him a sour look or, worse, stared vacantly at the TV turning his pleasure to dust.

"Summer is for people," he'd repeated, as if giving his friends another chance to dispute him. But he got no arguments, no quizzical looks. And nobody dared to remind him of the incident. He had Galena for that, with her vacant gaze, her shows, her Mr. Jan Peerce who once sang with the Bolshoi Opera.

The women remind him of colorful songbirds the way they perch on the picnic bench, bantering and laughing. They dress in bright sundresses and glittering costume jewelry, as if a gathering in the park were a great occasion. They fuss with their hair, doing it up in arrangements elaborate as birds' nests. Always, they ask, "So how's Galena?"

"Good. Good," he replies. "She's watching her show."

"What's so good she can't tear herself away, join us for an afternoon?" someone asks.

He's told them about Rex, the German shepherd who works with a Viennese police inspector. Galena watches *Kommissar Rex* with Russian voice-over. "That show is a miracle," Lev has wanted to say, but then Morris would counter, *Only peasants believe in miracles.* Still, Lev marvels at the cascade of events that led to the moment when a depressed woman in an eighth-floor apartment in Minneapolis can view a show filmed in Vienna, spoken in German, dubbed into Russian, and transmitted, via satellite, all the way from Tel Aviv. Their migration from Baku had been easier.

Lately, Lev has taken to asking Galena about the dog. "So, how is Rex?" Once, she told him that Rex had been shot, just as the show was ending. That evening, she picked at her supper. "You'll see," he'd said. "Everything will be okay. Rex is the star of the show. He can't die. Please, Galena. Go ahead and eat."

She watched other things, too. The TV, which consumed more than its fair share of space in the cramped living room, played a hundred channels, maybe more. It was a gift from Benjamin, who is too busy to tear himself away from his fancy job with that oil company in Houston. Galena revered the set as if it were Benjamin himself, and it practically is, the way she's arranged his pictures on top. A shrine to their only child.

Now, Lev mops up the yolk with a piece of bread, finishes off the fruit compote and consults his watch. He calls out to Galena, reminds her that it's Wednesday. It's the day they go to the community center to study *English for Newcomers*, though Galena hasn't attended class in months, and after fifteen years, neither of them can be considered a newcomer.

Last week, when Lev returned from class, Galena had changed out of her bathrobe into a blouse with a pattern of blue cornflowers. She had on pink slacks and lipstick to match. Her lunch plate sat empty on the coffee table in front of her. She looked up at him and smiled. When he asked how her morning had gone, she replied, "Good. Good." Lev took this as a positive sign. She'd replied in English, a habit their teacher encouraged, but which they rarely had the patience to practice. He beamed at his wife. She had not given up. Maybe she'd even return to class, meet the world half way. "Now," he'd said. "Let's have some tea."

Lev drank his tea from a tall glass, holding it near the rim so as not to burn his fingers. Before taking the first sip, he clamped a sugar cube between his front teeth, closed his eyes and waited for its sweetness to burst on his tongue. He'd pushed the sugar bowl toward Galena. When she refused, he said, "What's the matter with you? Take one. It's sweet." He plucked a cube from the bowl, set it on her place mat, before helping himself to another.

Absentmindedly, Galena stirred the sugar in her tea. She raised the cup, blew on it, then set it down without drinking. She stirred again, with the same air of distraction, but when she looked up, her eyes, blue as the flowers on her blouse, fixed directly on Lev. "They caught the criminal," she said.

He set his glass down. "But why didn't you tell me this? This is great news."

"I'm telling you now."

"When? Where? Do they want you to identify him? Tell me. Oh, Galena."

He recalled the police officer saying they'd have a hard time finding the man, though Lev had suspected nobody would bother to look. Dutifully, the officer had questioned Galena, jotting things on a notepad, but she had little to offer. In her agitation, she kept repeating, "My documents. My documents."

It had happened quickly. Her sister was recovering from the flu and Galena was heading over to Irina's apartment with breakfast. That morning, she'd taken a shortcut through the park. She thought she'd tripped on a rock or a branch, but then she understood that her purse was gone. Her left arm took the brunt of the fall. By afternoon it would be sheathed in a plaster cast. Before she could set her broken glasses back on her face, pigeons were attacking the Kaiser rolls for Irina's breakfast.

After Irina phoned looking for Galena, Lev raced to the elevator. In the lobby, he encountered great commotion. Donna, the building manager, stood clutching a little white dog to her breast. There was a young woman in jogging clothes, the one, he later learned, who had found Galena wandering dazed at the edge of the park. There were others he did not know. Finally, he saw Galena, swallowed up in the hubbub by a wingchair near the sliding glass doors. She was clutching her arm; her cheek was streaked with dried blood. And there was Solomon Polachek, talking first to Galena, then to a police officer, and then the other way around.

Intermittently, Mrs. Jensen from the third floor squawked like a parrot. "Was he black? Was he black?"

The officer, a handsome man with a gentle demeanor, shot Mrs. Jensen a look before tapping a finger to his cheek, saying, "If we were to stop every black man, we'd have to stop me." Turning back to Galena he said, "Isn't there anything you can recall, Mrs. Zarov?"

She stroked her arm and moaned, "My documents. My documents."

Lev stood watching from the sidelines, as if none of this pertained to him. Only after Mrs. Jensen pointed an accusing finger at him, as if he were the mugger, and said, "That's her husband," did Lev push his way through the crowd and kneel beside his wife. He whispered something in her ear and when she nodded, he looked up at the officer and explained that she had been referring to her citizenship papers, which she carried with her everywhere. He didn't volunteer that the original documents were in a shoebox in the back of the bedroom closet. If he did that, the police would never look for her purse. Or the mugger.

Twelve weeks later, Galena, dressed in her pink slacks and pretty blouse, said, "They caught the criminal."

Elated, but in a state of disbelief, Lev asked when she'd heard the good news.

"Just now," she replied.

"They just called?"

"What are you talking about? Nobody called."

"Oh, Lena. Lena. What are you talking about?"

She tugged at her arm, which bowed slightly at the wrist, as if she were trying to correct what the cast had failed to remedy. "Rex," she whispered, staring into her lap.

"Rex?"

She nodded and looked up at Lev. "He found the man who murdered the chef." She wrinkled her nose and said, "He smelled the rare wine. It was stolen. Rex has a good nose."

"Ah," Lev said, sinking back in his chair. "So it's Rex."

❉　❉　❉

Today when Lev returns from class the TV is off and Galena is sewing a button on his favorite blue shirt. "You still have the touch," he tells her. "Your fingers fly like hummingbirds."

"Is no good," she says, without looking up.

"If you say so," he says, thinking how their smallest exchanges deflate him. He probes her face for signs of the bright, capable woman he'd married. It was just after the war. She'd been sent from Leningrad to a coat factory in Baku, where he was teaching mathematics. She was a quick study, had a mind for detail, retained everything. Soon she was assisting the designer of women's coats, overseeing the cutting, the alignment of zippers and buttons, the snipping of loose threads.

Now, as she sews on the button, Lev fills her in on news from the class. They have a new teacher, a pretty young woman with a soft voice and a loud laugh. She hands out stories from *People*, stories about movie stars and rock singers, abducted children and train wrecks. Today, a student raised her hand and asked if they might read Chekhov. "The teacher said, 'Chekhov?' as if, suddenly, she's the one learning a new language," Lev tells Galena. "So the student says, 'In English, of course. We can read Chekhov in English.' Still, the teacher looked puzzled and that's when I understood that she had never heard of the great master."

Lev shakes his head as he fixes his gaze on Galena, waiting for her to share his dismay.

"Rex," she says, as if by way of reply. "He helped the police solve another crime."

What were they doing, talking about a dog on TV? Recently, he'd said, "Galena, what's happened to you?" A look of terror crossed her face, as if they'd been at a street fair and he'd asked where three-year-old Benjamin had gone.

Now, as gently as his frustration allows, he tells her, "On TV, things get solved. In one hour, everything is better." Then, out of the blue, he hears himself saying, "Perhaps you'd like a dog." The idea surprises him. It sounds like an expression their teacher would have them learn—*Perhaps you'd like a dog*. Yet it sounds right.

"A dog?" She tests the button, then snaps the thread, jams the needle into the spool and thrusts the shirt at him. "Where would we put a dog?"

"I'm thinking something small, like the little white mutt Donna carries in her arms."

"Yes. A lap dog." She claps her hands together, in mock delight. "In the summers, we'll take it with us to the dacha. Oh, Lev. What would we do with a dog?"

❄ ❄ ❄

After dinner, Lev heads to the park. Everyone is there, crowded around the picnic table, chattering and laughing. When Morris Reznick brings up the teacher who hadn't heard of Chekhov, they all start talking at once, until someone says, "What are you going to do?" Everyone agrees and then they fall silent until one of the sisters says, "Has anyone seen Klara?"

"Poor Klara," Solomon Polachek says, and repeats what they already know, that last week Klara Kleinman had stood sobbing in front of the orange juice cooler at Cub Foods. "Too many juice," she cried, as the driver, who'd been waiting in the parking lot, escorted her back to the van while the others finished shopping.

Then Morris turns to Mr. Polachek. "What's so poor about her?"

Firmly, Natalia presses her husband's arm and says, "How soon you forget." She tells the others how, on their first trip to Target, Morris had stood staring at the toothpaste. "I said, 'Moishe. Make up your mind.'" Smiling at her husband, she says, "And what did you say?"

"I said, 'I could lose my mind before I decide. You decide.'"

Natalia beams at him. "Exactly."

"Yes, but I didn't break down and cry like a baby and refuse to ever leave my apartment."

"All the more reason to pity the poor woman," Natalia says.

If it wasn't for the fading sun, Lev might see six pairs of eyes darting nervously, one to the other. Still, he senses his friends' embarrassment. Pity the poor woman. The words pierce the soft evening air.

After an awkward silence, the conversation turns to the specials at Cub Foods. Last week, cherry tomatoes were on sale, two for one. This week it was blueberries. Larissa tells them she baked a blueberry babka.

"So where is it?" Mr. Polachek teases. "You don't share with friends?"

The truth is, they never carry food to the park. The park is for strolling, sitting on benches, talking, reading. Occasionally, Lev and Mr. Polachek play a friendly game of chess. There's no need to bring food outdoors. They have tables and chairs in their small apartments for that. Proper utensils. Dishes. Placemats. Yet blueberry babka in the park would be nice, they agree.

Others bring food. They eat on the run. Lev has observed people rushing through the park with briefcases and coffee cups. People amble along drinking water from plastic bottles or soft drinks in cans. The other day, Lev headed out after lunch, a book tucked under his arm, and discovered a group of scantily clad young people at his table. They'd piled it high with liters of soft drinks, bread in plastic bags, shrink-wrapped meats. Paper plates. During breaks from some game that involved the tossing of a red plastic saucer, one or the other broke away, ran to his table, grabbed something to eat, then quickly rejoined the group.

His table. Listen to that. Of course, he has no claim to it. Yet what is one picnic table among so many? Hadn't the early settlers been given land? One hundred and sixty acre tracts? True, with each successive wave of newcomers the parcels had grown smaller. Yet even his mother's brother, Leo Pinsky, who fled after the Kishinev Massacre, received a small plot of land somewhere outside New York. An agency had relocated him from the city, sent him to the countryside, told him to raise chickens, a cow. Compared to all that, what was one wooden table rooted to a slab of concrete by an iron chain?

"Gypsies," Lev had muttered, as he turned away with his book and searched for a bench in the shade. The next morning, it took an extra jug of water to clean the tabletop. ANARCHY. Someone had scrawled the word in mustard on the tabletop. It had baked in the sun, acquiring the permanence of the brilliant tattoos that snaked up and down the legs of those pishers. ANARCHY. What did they, with their scanty clothes, their plastic toys, their hot dogs and buns, know of anything? Two trips he'd made to refill the water jugs.

He can't recall when it started, but every day, Lev arises at dawn, eager to get to the park. He rises quietly, so as not to awaken Galena. In sleep, her face in calm repose, her faded blonde hair fanned out on the pillow, she appears as beautiful as the day he married her. Some days, she opens her eyes and wishes him a good morning. "Look at you," she'll say, "rising early to look after the land. A count out of Tolstoy."

Despite his silver hair, remarkably abundant for a man past his prime, Lev Zarov looks nothing like a Russian nobleman. His coloring is too florid. His costume is wrong. He favors hemmed

111

shirts with three-inch side vents that drape comfortably over his old-man's belly. In his leather sandals and dark socks, he could easily be mistaken for a German tourist.

Always before leaving, Lev leans over to kiss his wife's soft cheek and whispers, "Go back to sleep." Then, the self-appointed caretaker of a small plot of land on the edge of a public park, heads out with his tools. In winter, he carries a shovel to clear a path to the table. With a whiskbroom, he sweeps snow from the tabletop. The rest of the year, he carries a broom to sweep the sidewalk; he totes jugs of water to wash everything clean.

The casual observer might be excused for wondering whether this ruddy-faced man was a retired shop owner habituated to mopping his storefront sidewalk each morning. But in the old country Lev, the mathematics teacher, performed his daily ablutions by wiping the slate clean for the next day's lesson. Sometimes he'd pause, sponge poised in midair, marveling at the proofs and equations that filled the chalkboard, knowing that nothing in his life had ever been, or would ever be, as certain as those elegantly balanced truths.

A biker whizzing by brings Lev back to his companions. Nobody wants the velvet evening to end. Couples, arms linked, stroll past. More bikers appear. Playful shouts erupt from the basketball court. Dog owners are out for their final walk of the day. The chirring of late summer insects heralds nightfall. Only when the streetlights come on, do Lev's companions stir. The women, that bevy of songbirds, appear to rise at once. The men slowly follow. As the group disperses, someone reminds Larissa about the babka and she laughs.

❋ ❋ ❋

On sleepless nights Lev stands by the window with his binoculars. In letters home, he brags about the view. Our place is on the eighth floor of a high rise overlooking a beautiful park. He describes the pond where people skate in the winter. And in summer, the pond is home to egrets and herons and even wood ducks. Parents take children to fish off a dock by the reeds. He describes the formal garden and a fountain that sprays water like dandelion seeds in the wind. Children splash in the fountain, shrieking with joy. Like children everywhere. Lev's letters omit any reference to the boisterous young men who lay claim to the basketball court, their t-shirts tossed casually to the ground, disconcerting him with their lack of inhibition. He doesn't write about the other men either, the ones who camp out under the trees or sleep on the benches. Nor does he reveal that his rent is heavily subsidized, so once again he is a dependent of the state. He doesn't write that his building is managed by a Christian charity and that to reach the elevator he must pass a table upon which rests an enormous New Testament, opened to a different passage each day. In the elevator hangs a picture of Jesus wearing a crown of thorns. There are notices in English and Russian about daily prayer services, amateur musical performances, social hours. Recently, a note appeared warning the women to avoid carrying handbags in the park.

Now, from his eighth-floor aerie Lev surveys the park. Does he really expect to discover the mugger, even with binoculars? Galena's incredible Rex would have trouble finding such a man. Lev has told her as much. "Your arm is healed. And you've got your documents. Your purse. Not even Rex can do better. It's over, Lena. Let it be."

He is beginning to comprehend that her mood suits her. Darkness is her companion, her balm. Her revenge. It is her way of saying that he may as well have carted them off to the moon. But they had to leave. The day he returned home, after louts knocked him down in the street, he'd told her, "Enough is enough. We're leaving." She'd replied, "The tension won't last. This sort of thing has always been the case. Do you think it will be any better in America? Nobody likes the Jews." The irony had not been lost on him. He hadn't needed to remind her that years ago the state had robbed them of their religion. In Baku, a place that forbade him to be a Jew, he was tormented for being a Jew. And hadn't her father, a rabbi, been taken away in the middle of the night by Stalin's henchmen? "You're right," he'd replied. "Nobody likes us. But this is a civil war and we're caught in the middle, fair game for either side. It will be different over there. You'll see." And then they were in Italy, in limbo, waiting for visas. Six months they lived, packed together with another family in a drab hotel room, between the only world they'd ever known and the world to come. Sponsors awaited them in Minneapolis, distant relatives willing to vouch for them. "You'll feel at home here," the cousins had written. "Bring warm clothes." Warm clothes they had.

Now, bringing the binoculars into focus, Lev spots a tall, heavy-set man circling the picnic table. Suddenly, the man pauses and looks around, as if sensing that someone is watching. Then he hops up and sits, resting his heavy boots on the very spot where, earlier in the evening, Larissa had set her pleasing round bottom. In the morning Lev will go out with his water and rag and scour the bench. He'll collect whatever the man leaves in his wake. Styrofoam cups, cigarette butts, potato chip bags, candy wrappers, chicken bones, beer cans, plastic bags, vodka bottles. Lev has seen it all. Once, in the middle of a heat wave, he found a sticky condom.

Even with binoculars, Lev has trouble reading faces. He guesses the oaf is thirty. Despite the heat, he is wearing a jacket, the kind Lev has seen in the window of the Army surplus store on Nicollet. His hair falls to his shoulders, in a strawberry blond cascade, like a vision out of Renoir. Lev should wake Galena, ask her to take a look. Is this him? Did he have hair like a young girl? A soft beard to match? His jacket. Does it look familiar? But she already told the officer everything she'd seen, which was nothing. Lev adjusts the binoculars. Without hesitation, he can identify a Horsfield's cuckoo. Once, in the Astrakhansky forest, he spotted a Eurasian three-toed woodpecker. But Galena's mugger? There are no field guides for such things.

The young man pulls something from his pocket, tilts his head back, and after taking a swig, wipes his mouth with the back of his hand. He sits motionless for the longest time, then suddenly slides off the table and staggers toward a tree, the very one Mr. Polachek had exclaimed over that evening. With a dramatic bow to the tree, Mr. Polachek had said, "For the gift of your shade, we thank you," and the sisters chimed in, "Amen!"

The man faces the tree for a long time, like Lev, who can stand forever and hardly anything comes out. But at thirty, even forty, Lev had not been beset by such problems. Now Lev sees that this man suffers from nothing worse than a full bladder. He pisses like a horse. He is drowning their tree. Lev wants to shout at him to stop, that he is killing it. But his voice would never carry and for once, Galena is sleeping soundly.

Lev tiptoes out of the apartment, carrying a water jug and his sandals, slipping into them when he reaches the lobby. He exits through the sliding glass door into the still, summer night.

Galena would call him crazy for what he is about to do—confront a stranger, in the middle of the night. But Lev approaches his table without hesitation, greeting the young man with a solemn nod, an Old World formality that suggests the doffing of a cap.

"Whoa," the young man cries, leaning back, as if to create distance between him and Lev. "You scared the hell out of me, man."

By way of reply, Lev holds up the plastic jug.

Warily, the man shakes his head and pats his pocket. "I've got my own," he says. "So why don't you go find yourself another table? This park is big enough for the two of us. Did you hear me? I said, 'Find another table.' Amscray. Scram. Vamoose. Take a hike."

Lev tries speaking, but his tongue is thick, useless. His mind scrambles to recall if the teacher has taught them such words. Scram. Vamoose. Finally, he says the first thing that comes to mind. "Is my table."

The man tilts his head to one side and cups a hand to his ear. "Say what?"

Calmly, Lev repeats, "Is my table."

"Your table?" The man slaps his thigh and laughs. "Your table. That's rich. This is a public park. As in public." He spells out the word.

In the light of the full moon, Lev sees that the man is not yet thirty. He's practically a child, perhaps the age Lev's prize pupil, Anatoly, would be today. But Anatoly had worn crisp shirts with starched collars. Polished boots. Anatoly looked you in the eye when he spoke. This strange man's eyes focus on nothing as they dart nervously about.

116

Again, Lev holds up the jug, this time making a beeline for the tree where the man had relieved himself.

The man calls after him. "Did somebody send you here to torment me? Are you like some angel in reverse? Or perhaps I forgot to take my meds. I must be seeing things. As in hallucinating." He spells hallucinating.

Lev is sloshing water over the desecrated ground when the man suddenly rushes toward him, shouting, "What the F?"

Lev continues to ignore him, the way he had years ago, when Josef Paretsky barged into his classroom after school, overturned a desk, lunged at Lev and threatened to choke him if he didn't receive a passing grade. Back then, like now, Lev should have been afraid, but a feeling had swept over him—something between resignation and acceptance—a feeling Josef must have sensed, for suddenly the student collapsed to the floor and begged forgiveness.

Now, finished with the tree, Lev helps himself to some of what's left in the jug, then offers it to the man.

"Thanks, but no thanks," the man mutters. After hoisting himself back on the table, he pulls the bottle from his pocket and between swigs, chatters fast as a mynah bird. Lev, who is mentally composing the things he wants to say, can hardly keep up. At last, the man pauses for a drink and Lev breaks in. "My wife." He forgets what he'd planned to say next. "My wife. My wife," he stutters. And then it comes to him. "She is knocked down. In street." He points to a spot not thirty meters from where he stands. "She breaks arm. Now, she sits with TV. All day, the television. She thinks dog will find man who knocked her. She talks about dog. And she says to me, 'I am suffering for my arm.'"

"Whoa!" The man holds up both hands. "I'm beginning to get your drift and I do not like it. Not one bit. I am here to tell you that you are barking—Hah! No pun intended—up the wrong tree."

Lev shifts his weight from one foot to the other, clutching the water jug and staring at the man's mouth, waiting for something, anything, to fly out that he can grasp. Barking up wrong tree. Was the man talking about dogs barking? Everywhere, all Lev hears is dogs. Lev nods. "You like dogs?"

"Oh, Holy Je-sus Christ." The young man rakes a hand through his remarkable hair. "What planet are you from? I don't have to be Sherlock Holmes to know you're not from here." He leans forward, trying to stare Lev down, but his darting eyes betray him.

Lev stands, unflinching, the way he'd faced his angry student, while the young man shouts, "Where. Are. You. From?"

"Ah. Yes." Lev sighs with relief. "Baku."

"Bak what?"

"Baku. Is in Russia. Soviet Russia. Now, no," he says, wagging a finger for emphasis. In Russian, Lev could talk for hours about the breakup of the Soviet Union, the independence of Azerbaijan. The ensuing civil war. The ethnic strife. But he is reduced to broken sentences and finger gestures. Without the means of self-expression, he is trapped inside himself, lost in translation.

"I knew it." The young man slaps his thigh and grins. "You're not from here."

Not from here. That, Lev understands. After all these years, he is still not from here. He is still a student of English for Newcomers.

For a long moment, Lev waits for the man to say more, but he is busy with his bottle, which, after a long swig, he holds out to Lev.

Lev shakes his head and again hoists the jug.

"Oh, come on," the man pleads. "Try this. Fire water. Much better than your brand." He practically topples over as he extends it to Lev, who understands this much: to refuse is an insult.

In the distance, Lev hears the faint call of a barred owl. When it stops, he gestures for permission to sit on the bench. The young man slides over, and once seated, Lev takes an audible breath. On the exhale, he repeats what he'd told his friends. "Summer is for people."

The wild-eyed man hoots with laughter. "That's the funniest thing I've heard all day. 'Summer is for people.'" Bemused, he shakes his head. "Actually, these are the dog days. So you could say, 'Summer is for dogs.' But that's not right, either. You know, people get it wrong about the dog days. They think it refers to summer days that are so hot even dogs won't do anything but laze around. Now the Romans. They had the right idea. They associated hot weather with the star Sirius, which they considered to be the Dog Star, because it's the brightest star in the constellation *Canis Major*. That's Latin for 'large dog.'" He pauses, takes a swig, then tosses the empty bottle to the ground. "I bet you're wondering what the 'h' 'e' double 'l' I'm saying. And if you knew, you'd wonder how I came to know all that I know. And I would tell you, 'That's for me to know and you to find out.' Hah! But I will tell you that you've given me something to think about. Summer is for people. That sounds like one of those Zen riddles."

The man prattles on making so little sense that even Lev's teacher of English would have trouble understanding. He doesn't stop, not even when he lies down, resting his head at the end of the table where Mr. Polachek had earlier in the day talked about the fires consuming Moscow this summer.

Lev remains seated while the strange, young man talks himself to sleep. Soon, a soft, guttural snoring replaces his ragged breathing; his eyelids flutter shut, and his face rearranges itself into something close to contentment. Even the manic eyes have come to rest beneath heavy lids. Gently, Lev raises the collar on the man's jacket to shield him from the night air. *"Dasvidaniya,"* he whispers. Then he reaches under the table for the empty bottle. Polish. Like the one he'd collected this morning. Yesterday morning, by now. *"Dasvidaniya."* Then he starts for home.

As he steps through the sliding glass door, Lev again recalls the teacher explaining, Doors will open for you. "It's an idiom," she'd said. Once, during a different lesson, Lev had raised his hand and asked, "Is that, too, an idiot?" She laughed so hard, Lev never asked another question. Let the others disgrace themselves, like that blockhead Zaretsky, always with his hand in the air. "Teacher. I don't understand. How can a door open for you?" That's when Lev almost blurted, *What difference does it make?* They needed to know how to get on the right bus, ask directions, explain to the store manager that when you got it home the milk was sour. They needed, it now occurs to him, to be able to describe, in as much detail as possible, the distinguishing features of the man who knocked you down in the park, stole your purse, broke your wrist. Crushed your soul. Still, Lev understands the idiom. Not that doors had opened for him, as they had for Benjamin, their son. Or for Boris, the *shtarker*. Yes. Lev's big shot nephew Boris has a house in the suburbs with a redwood deck and an outdoor grill that is larger than the kitchen stove

Galena cooks on. The younger ones have it easy. Boris. Benjamin. They picked up the language; they blended in.

Lev waits for the elevator knowing that in a few hours it will be morning. He will return to the park with his water and broom. The young man will be gone. Galena will settle in to watch her shows and applaud like a child when Rex solves another case. Later in the day, Larissa, to everyone's delight, will bring blueberry babka. They will eat off paper plates. Just like Americans.

Caves of Lascaux

I**T ISN'T EASY BEING THE BEARER OF BAD NEWS. STILL, LAWR** Marks prides himself on knowing which patients can handle the unadulterated truth, and which ones would prefer being left in the dark. He knows how to dole out information in increments, giving his patients time to process a new reality. He offers statistics only when asked, and he always tries to make the patient sitting in front of him feel as if she is the one the odds will favor. But when he broke the news to Nora Hill, he felt as green as he had the very first time he'd looked a woman in the eye and said, "You have breast cancer."

He wanted to tell her, "You should be out dancing the samba until the sun comes up." Instead, he informed her that her left breast would have to go.

He remembers the way her thick, black hair was pushed back with a simple tortoise shell headband. Other than a splash of red lipstick, her face was unsullied by makeup. To conceal such beauty would be a waste, and he was grateful that she seemed to know that.

Lawr won't easily forget the date, which was two years ago, and not just because it is recorded in a medical chart, or because on October 15, after nearly twenty years of practicing medicine, he lost his professional bearings. It happened also to be the day he drove right past Angie's Stems and Vines without stopping to pick up the primrose bouquet he'd ordered for his wife, Selma, for their eighteenth anniversary.

He remembered the flowers only after he walked through the front door, smelled rosemary and garlic in the air, and saw a bottle of champagne chilling in a silver ice bucket. The table had been carefully laid out as only Selma, a gourmet caterer, could do. While she had been preparing a celebratory dinner, he'd been wondering whether Nora Hill was aware of how beautiful she looked without any makeup.

Lawr tiptoed back out the door and returned to Angie's to pick up the flowers, calling Selma from the car to say he'd been detained. He told himself that anybody could have forgotten, even the president of the Lincoln Park Hosta Society, even Dr. Green Thumb, as Selma calls him. Besides, hadn't he remembered that primrose, nearly impossible to get at this time of year, was Selma's favorite? But hard as he tried to picture his wife's pleasure as she arranged the bouquet in a crystal vase, he could only see Nora's face, hear the sound of her voice.

"I guess it's my turn now," Nora had said. Lawr kept a box of tissues handy for such occasions, but it was clear she wouldn't need them. Her posture remained erect; her hands stayed folded in her lap as she absorbed the news.

"Nobody should have a turn at forty-three," he'd wanted to say, but experience had taught him that silence was often better than rushing to fill the void.

It wasn't until Nora said, "So now what do we do?" that he sensed he was in trouble. Never before had the first person plural sounded so much like foreplay. This wasn't the first time that Lawr had to confront a patient with such grim news, but it was the first time he stumbled over his own desire. That's when his eyes moved to her left hand, searching for a band of gold. So there is a husband, he thought.

The truth was, in a case like Nora's there wasn't much that could be done and he had to press his hand into his thigh to keep his foot from shaking. Then he tried to calmly lay out the game plan, which included a six-month course of chemotherapy, followed by radiation treatments. Lawr didn't say that within six weeks she'd have no need for the tortoise shell headband, and that by eight, she would have to pencil in the arch of her eyebrows, that he so desperately wanted to touch. The rosy color would drain from her cheeks, and dark hollows would appear beneath her eyes. Her blood would thin and her appetite would wane, though food was the very thing she would need the most. After all that, she would die anyway.

Now, two years have passed, and she's still alive. But as Lawr taps on the examining room door, he knows that Nora Hill won't live long enough to acquire cataracts or osteoporosis or any of the other ordinary diseases of aging.

Nora is perched on the table, draped in a flimsy paper gown that rustles as she looks up. She looks good today. Her cheeks have color, though that could be a sign of nothing more than a few deft strokes with a makeup brush, something the hospital teaches, along with the artful tying of scarves.

Nora is a long way from needing the tortoise shell headband, yet enough hair has grown back that it looks deliberate, even chic.

For a moment, Lawr fools himself into thinking that she has rounded a corner. When her hair grows long again, he will buy her the red velvet headband he saw on a mannequin in the window at Marshall Field's.

"*Bonjour!*" he booms. The greeting, which sounds hollow today, has become part of their routine ever since Nora announced that she was going to France. She and her husband had planned the trip when her cancer was in remission, and during checkups, while he palpated her remaining breast, searched for lumps under her armpits and around her clavicle, she talked about going to see the prehistoric cave drawings at Lascaux. There would be a side trip to Bilbao to the new museum everyone was talking about. "The one Frank Gehry designed," she'd explained. She planned to eat foie gras and walnuts. "The region is famous for walnuts, Dr. Marks. I bet you didn't know that."

By then, her flesh hung from her skeleton like a loose-fitting silk kimono. Still, when he warned her in his most authoritative voice to watch those calories, her eyes lit up, as if at last she had an ordinary health concern. But despite the remission, he knew she wouldn't have to watch her weight. He'd seen it before. The cancer was taking a time out, gearing up for its final assault.

"*Bonjour,*" she croaks back. Her voice is weak, but he's glad to see that her toothy smile hasn't changed. How many times had he pictured her sinking those perfect teeth into a freshly picked apple? At what point had he imagined her transferring such affections to his lower lip? Was it before or after he'd met her husband?

William Hill, a quiet, gangly man, has never looked Lawr in the eye or questioned him about his wife's condition. When Nora reported that William had dropped out of the cancer center's support group, after just one visit, Lawr wanted to take her in his arms and console her. In a fatherly way, of course, though they were about the same age. Once in his arms, their lips would meet. No harm in a simple kiss. Then he thought of Selma. In all these years, he's never strayed.

Now Nora hands him a piece of paper. "What's this?" he asks.

"The trip is off," she replies.

"And this is some sort of proclamation?"

She attempts a smile. "I bought trip insurance. You have to tell them why I can't go."

He glances at the paper without reading it. What would he write? Patient is too weak to travel? Patient is dying?

He looks up and sees Nora's eyes fixed on him. They are as green as the hostas he propagates in his spare time. Eyes like hers were meant to feast upon the wonders of the world. This is a test, he thinks. You can lie to me, her eyes are saying. But you cannot lie to Lloyds of London.

"Why wouldn't you go?" he asks, as he returns the form. Only this time he avoids her gaze.

At lunch, Lawr runs into Jack Robinson in the hospital cafeteria. Jack is sitting alone wolfing down the remains of a cottage cheese and canned peach salad. Lawr looks at the cheeseburger and fries on his own tray and wonders if he can escape unnoticed to another table. He should be the one eating the fruit plate. Selma has been testing new recipes on him and it's beginning to show. Last night, after they made love, she gently tugged the roll of flesh around his waist. "Look, Lawr," she laughed, as if she were pleased in having produced a bit more of him. "Love handles." Then she kissed him there and said she would love him no matter what. He started to say he would always love her too, but stopped short and wondered what was happening to him.

Let Jack raise an eyebrow, Lawr thinks as he sits down. Today he needs the comfort of a cheeseburger, a balm to soothe the uneasy feeling that has settled over him.

There is something different about Jack. It isn't the starched white shirt with the monogrammed cuffs, or the expensive gold watch. There is an air about him. Rumors circulate from time to time. Stories involving nurses. Jack has the kind of bad boy reputation that follows some men through life.

"Going somewhere?" Jack leans over and taps the travel brochure on Lawr's tray.

"Oh, this." Lawr slides it across the table, but overshoots and it lands near Jack's feet. "Just something I found in the waiting room. Gives me ideas, though."

In fact, Lawr picked up the brochure on a day when he'd resolved to spend his lunch hour walking. He stopped at a travel agency, telling himself that he wanted to surprise Selma with plane tickets to some exotic destination for their twentieth anniversary. The truth is, they only spend two weeks every summer at an A-frame on the North Carolina coast. Lawr doesn't like sleeping in strange beds. And he doesn't like to be away from his plants for long.

Suddenly, he has a desire to blurt it all out, as if Jack were a priest, not a retinal surgeon. Lawr wants to ask Jack if he's ever fallen in love with a patient. "Not a nurse," Lawr would say. "Ten minutes in the linen closet with a woman who isn't your wife, doesn't count."

Instead he says, "Ever been there?"

"Where?" Jack pops the last of the peach in his mouth, then consults his watch.

"South of France. People go to see the caves."

"I've heard of those. Prehistoric, or so they say. Could be a hoax." Jack points to the brochure, to a picture of a bison painted on a cave wall.

"Hoax?" Lawr says, though now he sees that it's a crude rendering, like a child's crayon drawing. "Why would anyone want to do that?"

"Why do we do anything?" Jack shrugs. "Money."

Lawr hates Jack at that moment. "Love, too!" he blurts.

"Say what?"

"Love," Lawr insists. "People do things for love, you know."

Jack checks his watch again, then rises.

"Hey, Jack! One more question, before you go."

Jack starts to set down his tray, but seems to think better of it. "What's that?"

"Ever fall in love with a patient?"

Now Jack does set down his tray, as if the question demands all of his energy. "Against the rules," he says, his voice tinged with remorse.

"But it could happen? Right?"

"Anything could happen." Jack sounds impatient. "The sky could fall."

After lunch, Lawr's nurse greets him with a sigh and a nod toward the crowded waiting room. Ignoring her, he shuts his office door, slumps in his desk chair, and riffles through a pile of pink message slips without reading them.

He looks up at the closed door. The faithful await him. They are too trusting. They are too willing to follow his advice. They consume whatever he prescribes. Poison. That's what he offers, like some sicko who laces Milky Ways with arsenic at Halloween.

"Faker," he whispers, looking at his hands, which are beginning to shake. "Charlatan." If only his patients knew how little he understood, they would be rushing across the border for laetrile. "Go to Mexico!" he wants to shout. "Consult a faith healer. Try that shark cartilage they sell over the Internet."

Lawr reads the pink slips. Selma has called three times. He starts to dial the number, then puts down the phone. He picks it up again and dials Nora. He has dialed her number before, only this time he lets it ring.

If she picks up, he will apologize for lying. But did he really lie? Why shouldn't she go to France, to see the Caves of Lascaux? And why shouldn't he accompany her? The Queen of England travels with a personal physician. He imagines an entire team on alert, waiting to defend against the slightest fibrillation of the Queen's heart, the shallowest breath. He will do the same for Nora, only he will make it seem like a chance encounter.

He is about to hang up when Nora's voice apologizes for not being able to take the call. "We." He's sure she said, "we," the very word that first triggered his desire. He dials again. "I'm sorry we cannot take your call."

Had he really forgotten about the husband? Or was he deluded by his own fantasy that William Hill was dead, the victim of a botched mugging or a drive-by shooting? Lawr has even imagined the mourners whispering, clucking, reveling in the delicious irony of the situation: the dying wife attending the healthy husband's funeral.

There is a knock at the door. It's his nurse, once again using her head to indicate a packed waiting room. When she leaves, he calls Selma, who asks him to stop off for a loaf of bread on his way home. She launches into a lengthy explanation as to why she can't do it, only he isn't listening. Then he redials Nora's number, pleased to know that he can conjure the sound of her voice whenever he wants.

❋ ❋ ❋

Lawr pecks Selma on the cheek and offers to run back out and pick up the bread. "Don't bother," she says, returning his kiss. She smells good, like burned sugar and lemons.

"*No problema.* Honest," he says, raising his right hand. This may be the truest thing he's said all day.

"*No problema,*" she protests. "I don't even know why I asked. There's plenty without it." She brushes a shock of hair off his forehead as she expresses concern for his day. She's letting him off the hook, though she'd called three times.

If only Selma knew that he had been too preoccupied with thoughts of France to remember a "silly old loaf of bread." If only she'd get angry. They could argue. He could storm out of the house. Then he could begin to build a case for taking a trip alone. A medical conference is what he has in mind.

Dinner is superb. Selma has prepared pumpkin soup, a new version of chicken marbella, and fennel salad with figs and oranges. He tells her the truth, that she could offer this meal to her clients and they will clamor for more. She tells him that the contents of a caterer friend's refrigerator is on the cover of *Chicago,* as part of a feature on the city's hottest caterers, a status that Selma aspires to as well. And she tells him that his mother called. "She wants us to visit. 'A week in Boca will do you good,' she said. And I said, 'You know Lawr doesn't like to travel.'"

He takes a sip of wine and clears his throat. How can he propose a trip now? But a medical conference is different. He will reassure her that he'd love to have her come along, but he understands this is her busy season.

Selma doesn't give him a chance. She wants to discuss his hosta. "I think I know why it's dying," she declares.

"Nothing is dying," he snaps.

"It is, Lawr. Don't you remember? You told me. Last week."

"You misunderstood. I said it *could* die, if I don't nurse it along." The truth is, it is dying, despite his best efforts. *Reversed*. It's a jokey name, given to a plant that seems to get smaller by the year. It's hard to germinate and even harder to keep alive. Selma knows it's his pride and joy. He refuses to admit that he can't make it grow.

"I stand corrected." She sighs, pushes the food around on her plate with a fork, a habit that drives him crazy, especially since she brings so little of it to her mouth. "In any event," she continues, "I think I know why it could be dying." Then she launches into a discussion of feng shui, her latest passion. She has already told him that according to feng shui, the proper placement of doors and windows, and even the arrangement of everyday household objects, can bring health, wealth, and happiness. "Your plant is facing the wrong direction," she declares.

"That's ridiculous. Why don't you just stick to the cooking, and leave the ailing plants to me?" He drains the last of his wine, refills

132

his glass, offers to fill hers, but she has already jumped up to clear the dishes. Her voice bristles as she tells him to stay put. Gone is the wife who forgave him for arriving home empty-handed.

Yet she's given him an opening. One pointed remark and the hurt on both sides will escalate, until he has his excuse to storm out the door. But he'd planned to head downstairs after dinner, to check on his seedlings, adjust the grow lights. Maybe he will even move the *Reversed* to a different part of the room.

He hears Selma humming as she clatters around the kitchen. She is incapable of holding a grudge, and he remembers how he loves her for that. Perhaps this is all I need, he thinks, as he pours the last of the wine. Even the love handles he's been fretting over don't seem so bad. Consider them ballast, he tells himself. Selma's cooking is keeping him grounded, on an even keel.

When Selma returns, she sets a picture-perfect dessert before him. *"Voila!"* she chirps.

"What have we here?" he asks, leaning toward it, as if to inhale a summer bouquet.

Selma shrugs and offers a close-lipped smile as she pierces the glazed surface with a silver knife. She will make him guess. She expects him to know the difference between a torte and a tart.

As he takes the first bite, her eyes are fixed on him, much as Nora's were when she tried to discern the truth about her condition. His feeling of contentment evaporates. He must say something now; a mere "delicious" won't suffice. If that's all he offers, Selma is likely to say, "The crust is a little on the tough side, don't you think?" The dessert has a nutty taste, though he doesn't know what to call it. "You've outdone yourself, Selma," he says.

"You don't think it's too sweet?"

He imagines Nora sitting across from him in some cozy French bistro, unapologetically scraping the last crumbs of a walnut tart from her plate, telling him her plans to start baking when she returns home. She will joke about entering a bakeoff. "And I'll win!"

"I got the idea for the torte from the brochure I saw on your desk in the study," Selma says, breaking into Lawr's thoughts. "The one with the picture of the French caves. It said the region is home to an annual walnut festival. Then I was flipping through the latest *Bon Appetit* and *voila*! A recipe for walnut tart."

Lawr doesn't know if he can take one more *voila*! Is she taunting him? Is she letting him know that she can read his mind? The walnut tart now strikes him as a rebuke of sorts.

Of course she can't read his mind. But there she is, leaning across the table, saying, "Are you planning a trip, Lawr?" as she sticks her fork into his tart.

"A trip? What gave you that idea?"

"The brochure. With the caves. On your desk. I figured maybe you were planning something. Are you?"

He reaches across for her wine. He feels her eyes on him. She is waiting.

He will tell the truth, but first he sips some wine. One more drop might drown out the reverberating sound of his own lies. But why wouldn't you go? Medical conference. Nothing is dying. A trip? Faker. Charlatan. Liar.

Selma is mashing the tart on her plate with the back of a fork. Waiting.

What can he say? The truth is, he can't keep his plants alive.

He poisons his patients. He has nothing to offer a dying patient but permission to see the world before it's too late.

Selma is still staring at him. She looks beautiful. The flickering candlelight highlights her perfect cheekbones. Her elbows are propped on the polished table; her chin is propped in her hands. He has an urge to move to her side and rest his head in her lap. He wants her to stroke his hair again, push it back off his forehead, express concern for his day. But she is waiting.

"I don't know," he whispers. "I just don't know." That's the best he can offer. That is the truth.

Subtle Variations

I F ONLY SELMA HAD SAID, *I DON'T DISLIKE CATS. I LOATHE THEM* (True). She wouldn't now be looking after Goldie's cat. But honesty is so overrated, which is more or less what she'd said to Lawr the other day. "You know, there's something to be said for white lies." He'd just taken an index finger to the sagging flesh at her jaw line, prodded it as if stuffing it into place, and gazed at her as he might when assessing the condition of one of his patients. Then he turned away, something she might have done at the market after rejecting overripe peaches or tomatoes. Fifty-six years old and that's what she's become—an old tomato. She'd only asked how she looked. He might have said: *Darling, you look terrific!*

Now as Selma calls for the cat, she considers all the things she might have told Goldie. *I have to wash my hair.* (Hackneyed lie.) *I have to water Lawr's hostas.* (Pants-on-fire lie.) *I'm busy.* (True actually.) But nobody is too busy to feed a cat, especially one that resides (somewhere) in the house next door. She might even have suggested that Goldie ask Lawr, only he's out searching for a bird, specifically

137

a warbler that nests in the new growth forests of western Michigan. In the end, Selma could neither tell the truth nor think of a lie white enough to sound convincing.

"Here kitty, kitty!" (She's forgotten its name.) "Come and get it. Kibble for kitty." She knows it's here. It tracks grit from the litter box onto the kitchen table; it coughs up hairballs on the Persian rugs. Paper plates crusted over with dried up bits of the previous day's tinned food are further evidence of the cat's existence. Goldie left an exact number of tins on the kitchen counter, along with an equal number of plates. One per day.

Goldie is a precise, well-toned, high-maintenance sort who goes through the day toting a plastic water bottle like a toddler with a sippy cup. She makes Selma feel that she ought to floss more, or at least stand up straight. Currently, she's on an old Umbrian estate where olives are grown and pressed into oil, and yoga teachers and their minions—middle-aged women of means, yearning for something new—find refuge. "You should try it," Goldie had said, handing Selma a brochure. She'd just issued instructions about the tinned food and the water, even turning on the tap, as if Selma might draw her water from a well.

The kibble for some unfathomable reason is served in the bathroom off Goldie's bedroom. When Selma followed Goldie upstairs for kibble instructions, she saw angel wings, small, tentative tattoos emerging from beneath the thin straps of her Lycra top, etchings barely large enough to transport a warbler.

Having replenished the kibble, Selma picks a jar of cream off the bathroom vanity, unscrews the lid, holds it to her nose. It smells expensive. She dabs some on her face and regards herself in the mirror. "Old tomato," she says, frowning at her reflection. Then she pockets the jar. Goldie has so much stuff. Some of the clothes in her closet still have price tags.

Selma follows the sound of music to the bedroom and perches on the edge of the four-poster bed. A radio is tuned to a station playing something soothing. Brahms, she thinks. When Goldie said she'd leave it on—for company—Selma nearly thanked her. The radio, of course, is for the cat.

The room is done up in soft blues and grays, a faux rendering of Zennish bliss. The walls are dove colored; the cat's clawing tower carpeted in baby blue. The felted toys strewn across the plush carpet like dead mice are in various shades of gray. Some, she sees, are terribly mangled. The cat is here.

She calls for the cat as she crosses the room, then stops short, startled by the sudden appearance of—not the cat—but her own reflection. The mirror, (which doesn't lie), reveals a tall, slender woman in faded jeans and t-shirt, one Lawr brought back from the Everglades. He'd gone to see spoonbills, though an alligator is lazing on the shirtfront, as is a chocolate stain left over from a party she recently catered for the mayor. Her eyes are the same clear green that Lawr once called, "the color of envy." Her hair, cut like a Dutch boy's, falls neatly at her jaw line framing the dewlaps Lawr had so clinically prodded. She is barefooted, having obediently parked her shoes at the front door. (Goldie has rules.)

The mirror is on the closet door, which Selma opens on the pretense of looking for the cat. Goldie's clothes are arranged by color and function, as deliberate as the taxonomic sequence in Lawr's field guides. Blouses. Skirts. Dresses. Slacks. Short to long. Dark to light.

Shoes, toes pointing out, appear ready for action.

She slips a silk blouse off a padded hanger and tries it on. The sleeves are too short, the bodice snug, but her feet slide easily into a pair of blue satin mules, in which she parades around the room. Selma feels like an overgrown child trying on her dwarf mother's clothes, only she isn't a large woman and Goldie is merely compact. "Here kitty!" she mewls, as she flops onto the plush mattress, shoes and all, to wait the cat out.

Closing her eyes, she listens to Brahms and imagines Goldie asleep in her stucco casetta while Lawr tramps through a jack pine forest searching for a Kirtland's warbler. "It's rare," he told her. "Development, deforestation, indifference," he said, as if reciting the Deadly Sins. Cats, too, she thinks, though he already knows that they kill more than a billion birds a year.

She hopes he finds his rara avis. He can add it to his list, which is not to be confused with that odious other list that has wormed its way into the lexicon. The "fuck it" list, she calls it, as in, "Oh, fuck it, I'll never get around to doing that." She has a list of thats. Learning to play the banjo. Visiting the Pyramids. Doing a double axel. In no particular order. Perhaps she will add: coax a cat out of hiding.

Catering a party thrown by a man whose wife is ill may or may not make it onto her list. When William Hill phoned the other day, she said she'd let him know by the end of the week. Now getting back to William is on a list of sorts, a haphazard mental assortment of things she really must do: buy milk, replace front porch light bulb. Feed Goldie's cat.

Owning a cat is not on Selma's list, mental or otherwise. She's already done that. A college roommate brought home a stray. When the roommate departed, the cat stayed. Selma fed it. Occasionally, the cat rubbed up against her legs and purred. It felt good. Nobody had rubbed up against her in a very long time. When it ran away, Selma did not post signs. LOST. CAT. REWARD. She was broke. Besides, it wasn't lost. It ran away. Hey diddle diddle.

❅ ❅ ❅

When Lawr phones, Selma is in bed, leafing through a kitchen catalogue. She bolts upright, as if Lawr, who regards naps as indulgent, has caught her in flagrante. She combs a hand through her hair while he tells her that he'd seem a white-throated sparrow this morning. And a scarlet tanager. "Though neither for the first time," he sighs.

"Been there? Done that?" She asks if he's forgotten how he disparages people who, once they've seen a bird, rush off to record the sighting. Twitchers, he calls them. Playfully, she asks if he might be getting a bit twitchy?

Ignoring this, he eagerly declares, "I'm on a quest, Selma!"

Me too, she considers saying. I'm on a quest for a whisk. I lost mine. She can ask how one can lose a whisk and then insert some silliness about Goldie's cat running off with it. But then she pictures him, slightly stoop-shouldered, a shambling old Boy Scout, heavy binoculars looped round his neck, a battered field guide jammed into a pocket of his cargo pants. Yet he is buoyed by a particular enthusiasm, an innate curiosity. She wonders if she wants anything as much, if she's ever wanted anything as much as he wants to see that bird? A whisk doesn't count. Tenderly, she tells him, "I hope you find it."

She gets out of bed, crosses the room and peers out the window at the yard, which over the years has become a showcase for Lawr's hostas. It's a soothing landscape, though she'd resisted at first. "All the plants look alike. Green. Green. Green," she'd complained, when he started the garden. She'd wanted bursts of color. Blowsy zinnias. Plump hydrangea. Fussy dahlias. "But the garden is in shade," he quietly explained, leading her down a mossy path, pointing as he gave expression to various shades of green. Kelly. Jade. Silver. Reverently, he said, "There's one that verges on blue." Then he directed her attention to their texture and shape. And when he exclaimed over one that looked like a Spanish fan, she recalled the time he'd tried to explain the difference between a greater scaup and a lesser. She was moved by his appreciation of subtle variations. Still, she wanted flowers.

Now she tells him that William Hill called. "I told him that you are traveling, that Dr. Asrani is covering for you and that Dr. Asrani is very good."

"What did he want?" Lawr sounds surprised.

"He said, 'Actually, I'm calling to speak to you.' I joked that I'm a doctor's wife, not a doctor, and that I could get in trouble for practicing medicine without a license." The doctor's wife, people call her. Why does no one speak of Lawr as the caterer's husband?

Selma has grown accustomed to the ordinary indignities that come with being a doctor's wife—phone calls in the middle of the night; dinners interrupted by patients who have only to look up their number because Lawr refuses to be unlisted. After preparing too many dinners that withered in the warming oven, she started a catering business, preferring to cook for strangers guaranteed to show up on time.

She repeats the shtick about the doctor's wife, then waits for Lawr to reply, perhaps even chuckle. William had laughed, though it was a ragged sound, the sound of a New Year's Eve reveler, the sound of forced gaiety. But she can barely detect the slightest susurration of breath on the other end, as if Lawr is withholding even that. Tired of his silence, she explains that William asked her to cater a party. "He said his wife loves to cook, only she's ill."

Selma once catered a party for a woman who insisted all the food be white. "ARFID. Avoidant/Restrictive Food Intake Disorder," a clinical Lawr had explained, when she mentioned the odd request. Repelled by the idea, but needing the work, Selma came up with a menu of parsnip soup, Parmesan egg white soufflé, and cauliflower with béchamel. Blancmange for dessert. Another time, she catered a party at the schvitz, the old Russian bathhouse on Roosevelt Road, lately appropriated and tarted up by young hipsters whose grandfathers and great-uncles had sweated out their woes in the dense, punishing steam. But never before had she been asked to cater a party for one of Lawr's patients.

"Just how ill is William's wife?" she asks, her voice small and tentative.

"Her name is Nora," he bluntly replies, and she feels chastised, as if she's been caught riffling through his desk or opening his mail. Filching his patient. "How ill is Nora?" she says, making her voice go smaller.

There is little affect in his voice, or perhaps it is resignation she hears when he reveals that Nora's cancer had just come back. "Roaring back."

"And so you offered my services?" she asks, though she already knows the answer. She'd asked William if he'd seen her card on the bulletin board at the Jewel. When he said, "The Jewel?" she understood that he did not shop for groceries. "Your husband," William stammered. "Dr. Marks. He told me that you could help."

In the early years of their marriage, she'd expressed a keen interest in Lawr's patients, and he eagerly discussed them with her. Though she never met them, she felt buoyed by their remissions and took their setbacks to heart. She grieved, sometimes for days, when they died.

At some point she began to wall herself off from the sorrow. Was it after the bar mitzvah held in the hospital room of a patient whose remission ended a few weeks before the family would have celebrated at the synagogue? Lawr attended; Selma sent cookies and a honey cake. Then the daughter of a patient undergoing a bone marrow transplant died of alcohol poisoning following a night of drinking at a campus party, and Selma understood that cancer did not confer immunity from further misery or heartbreak. Sadness, like the disease, had a way of mutating out of control. She stopped asking Lawr about his patients. He stopped attending funerals, walling himself off, too. He became president of the Lincoln Park Hosta Society. In the evenings, instead of talking about his day, he told Selma about the seedlings he was propagating under grow lights in the basement; he railed against the rabbits that were making a salad of his favorite plants.

Now, struggling to keep the irritation from her voice, Selma says, "How could you?"

He clears his throat, then quickly reverts to silence. At home, this would be the moment he shrugs and leaves the room, not in anger, never in anger, but purposefully, as if he's been summoned to check on a patient or see to an ailing plant. Now, though, he would have to hang up to end their exchange, something that can only be done in anger. Lawr is not angry. But she is. He has brought down the wall they'd so carefully constructed. Nora. Nora. Nora. The name cuts through the air.

"You dragged a patient into our lives," she says. "And you offered me as the consolation prize. Really, Lawr. How could you?" The words, harsher than she'd intended, cut through the air like icy shards. She's gone too far. She's already pushed him into betraying a patient's confidence, into violating that inviolable code of conduct. Yet hadn't he brought her into it, too? Ménage a something, she thinks.

She is met with a silence so profound that she wonders if he has hung up. When he finally speaks, he ignores her question, as if it was merely rhetorical. "You'll do it, won't you?" he says, expectantly. "You'll take the job?"

Suddenly she knows that she will not—cannot—take the job. Because in the middle of death, there would be a party. But she needs to hang on to this hard-earned truth, and so she murmurs a vague demurral, one that he can ponder while tramping through the woods, chasing the elusive warbler.

"All right, then," he says, too brightly, as if the matter were resolved. "The group beckons. I'll call you tomorrow. *Mañana*, Selma!"

"Wait!" she cries. "Listen. He said something strange. He said, 'But I'll get the flowers myself.'" She pauses. "I've never seen him, but I had this image of a rather ungainly man—one who's never set food in a supermarket—going off to buy flowers. It's enough to make me take the job."

145

The silence on the other end is of a different quality. She realizes that Lawr has hung up, though not, she is sure, in anger. Left alone with her thoughts, she imagines William bringing home a stiff bouquet of carnations. Yellow or pink. The sort of cellophane-wrapped afterthought one finds near the supermarket checkout. Nora, confined to her bed, will be spared the sight, but the chiming of cutlery and the staccato outbursts of party laughter will reach her. Perhaps she'll worry about red wine sloshed on the carpet or chocolate ground into the rugs. No. She'll see that none of that matters and even regret the time she'd wasted fretting over such things. But the flowers, Selma thinks, looking out at Lawr's shade garden. The flowers will matter.

❀ ❀ ❀

The doctor's wife is sprawled out on her neighbor's muted duvet, in one of her neighbor's sweaters—gray cashmere with pearl buttons. Her neighbor's sandals—red peeky toes with wedge heels—remind her of a cardinal on a dull winter day, a brilliant burst of color that makes you glad to be alive. It occurs to her that she hasn't seen a cardinal in days. "Damn cat," she mutters, and just then a slight tremor ripples through the mattress as the cat springs onto the bed. Selma props herself up on an elbow and watches it slink around the foot of the bed on little cat feet. It is beautiful—a sleek, silver Siamese, with a luxurious tail. She'd rather it were mangy, its fur matted and dull. Warily they eye each other, until she is forced to turn away, struck by a pang of something that she recognizes as jealousy, which turns to horror and then self-loathing as she realizes that she has been comparing herself, feature by feature, to a cat. Shrilly, she demands to know where it has been. "Out cavorting with the birds?"

The little minx eyes her with disdain, then turns away and starts batting at a red shoe with its velvet paw. Selma taunts it, raising and lowering her foot, pulling back whenever it gets near. Soon enough, the cat loses interest and moves to the edge of the bed.

"Don't go," Selma says softly. "You just got here. If you stay, I'll tell you about my dream last night."

The cat freezes and peers over its shoulder at her with a pitying look. Then, strangely obedient, as if mistaking itself for a dog, it circles in place and drops down in all its glory, surrendering to the comfort of the soft duvet.

Selma relaxes back too, closes her eyes and begins. "In my dream," she says, "Lawr was saying that crows are smarter than dogs. Then I said, 'Cats are smarter than crows and dogs.'" She opens her eyes, looks at the cat for some sign of approval, but the cat is busy licking a paw. "Cats are smarter than crows and dogs," she repeats, trying to quell the knot of irritation taking hold in her chest as she realizes she is trying to please a cat. "Actually," she continues, "I don't really know if you are one whiff smarter than a dog or crow. That was only a dream. In my dream, I knew I was lying, and I didn't care. I told myself that people lie all the time. Politicians. Everyday sorts. There are even scientists who take money to bend the truth. 'The ice caps are not melting!'" The cat lifts its sleek head and gives her a baleful look and when it returns to its ablutions the knot in Selma's chest unravels and explodes. "You don't give a shit, do you?" she says. "But I'm telling you anyway, you little vixen," she says, making her voice go smaller. "While you're lolling around preening, licking your paws, or out killing songbirds, the ice caps are melting. Still, people will lie. And in time, the lie acquires the patina of truth. And that's no lie."

147

Exhausted by her outburst, she sinks into the bedding, closes her eyes and listens for the Brahms, but something brassy and percussive is playing, something too energetic to suit her mood. "The radio's for you, I hope you know," she says, sneering at the cat. "I hope you like it. Oompah. Oompah. Pah. Goldie is good to you. I hope you know that, too. Anyway, she'll be home tomorrow. You'll be glad to see her. Lawr will be home, too." Suddenly, she has an image of Goldie, spooning her compact self into Lawr as he traces the outline of an angel's wing with the same, deliberate finger he'd used to prod her own sagging dewlaps. She bolts upright, props her elbows on the mattress and looks squarely at the cat. "You don't suppose?" she says, when suddenly it springs to its feet and vanishes, no doubt tired of her neediness. "You're right," she sighs, flopping back down into the pillows. "That's a crazy thought."

If the cat were still here, she'd tell it that Lawr had asked her to join him. She'd gone with him once, on a day hike through a nature preserve. The guide, who'd promised an indigo bunting, stopped abruptly in a marshy bog and whispered, "Listen!" In the distance, a bird warbled. "That's it!" he exclaimed, cupping a hand to his ear, before urging the group to move on. So when Lawr invited her to search for the warbler, she said, "I prefer to stay home." (No lie.)

What is it that Lawr calls her? My creature of comfort, he says, as if mussing her hair. She thrives on constancy, relaxes into the familiar. She is comforted by the patina of age, the old soft shoe. Her baking pans are dimpled and nicked, her wooden spoons chipped. When she started reading *Anna Karenina*—for the third time—Lawr said: "Aren't you bored?" When she shook her head, he said, "But you know how it turns out," to which she replied, "And you know we all die, Dr. Marks. Yet you keep on tending the sick." At once she regretted the glib retort, recalling that during her second go-round with the book, he'd surprised her with a hosta, the *Anna Karenina*, a delicate variety with a mauve and white-striped bloom.

She listens now for the brassy music, hoping it will rouse her, but some chatty ask-the-expert call-in show is on now. Selma missed the question, which, given the reply, could have been anything—how to manage a truculent pet, whether to cater a party. "Life doesn't turn out for any of us as we plan," the expert (a pet whisperer, it so happens) is saying. And Selma thinks of William and Nora, their plans disrupted by a roaring recurrence of illness.

※ ※ ※

Lawr, who has been crouched over his plants, rises as Selma rushes across the lawn into his arms. He kisses the top of her head as she buries her face in his sweater, taking in the dampish redolence of the woods. Pulling away, she studies him in the late afternoon light, surprised, even after their brief separation, by his quiet, good looks— firm jaw, sandy hair, slightly overlapping two front teeth. He has an honest face, one that suits his calm, deliberate manner.

"I hadn't expected you 'til tomorrow," she says, then asks what time he'd arrived, how long he'd been in the garden? Did he ever see the bird? "I'm afraid I haven't fixed dinner. I've been feeding a cat," she says, with a dramatic shudder.

He pecks her cheek, says something about rain, that he just arrived, and no, he never did see the bird. "But at least my plants survived," he says, with a satisfied look toward the bed of hostas he'd been inspecting.

She is about to joke that it is all but impossible to kill a hosta when something stops her. All these years he's been fussing over these plants. His little patients, she calls them. Yet only now has it occurred to her that his devotion to this hearty species is because of that—they are hearty. They refuse to die. With a deep sigh, she says, "I'm glad you're home."

Later, over grilled cheese sandwiches he tells her he may have heard the warbler. "Then again, it may have just been from someone's app." He sips his beer and nods approvingly. "This is good," he says, saluting her with his mug.

He is content with so little. She loves him for that. Why isn't contentment contagious? she wants to ask. But he is unusually talkative. He tells her how everything feels so tentative. "Or do I mean elusive?" He looks at her pleadingly, as if he needs her to explain his feelings to himself. "Fragile. So in peril," he laments. He picks up his mug, then sets it down and frowns at his beer, as if he has reconsidered his diagnosis and it is no good, after all. "I feel so helpless," he says, looking up at her. "But what can I do?" This is about the bird's decline, she knows, though he could easily be speaking about Nora Hill. *Roaring back* is what he'd said. And then he involved her in this misfortune by offering her services. *Call Selma!* And when she'd asked why, he'd fallen into one of his long silences.

She looks at him across the table, across the flickering candles. (And why not? she'd laughed, when he said, Candles with grilled cheese?) Now the evening can play out either way. She could lean over, take his hand, coo some reassurance, white lie that things aren't so bad, that the peril is all in his head. The ice caps are not melting! The birds are on vacation! Or her darker side could win out.

It is the latter that triumphs, and in a burst of righteous indignation, she says, "Whatever were you thinking?" Still smarting from his earlier evasions, she glares at him, challenging him with her eyes as well.

"Thinking?" Confusion clouds his face and she wishes her better angels had prevailed. Then he lets out a tiny yelp of understanding. "Ah! William. I suppose this is about him." He clears his throat, then fixes his sad gray eyes on her. "He found a lump in his breast and made an appointment to see me."

She listens with great attention, her anger ebbing as he explains that the lump was fatty tissue. "When I told him it was nothing to worry about, he apologized for taking my time. I said it happens all the time, and he said, 'What happens all the time? Other husbands have sympathetic malignancies? Or women mistake fatty tissue for cancerous lumps?'" Looking down at his plate, he tells her, "I didn't know what to say. And that's when he mentioned the party, one that he and Nora had been planning for some time." Returning his gaze to her, he says, "Before her cancer came back."

Seconds pass before she can speak. Haltingly, she says, "I can't stop thinking about her. About Nora." Nora. Nora. Nora. She pauses, waiting for the name to stop ringing in her ears, echoing through the air, bringing down the wall she, no they, had built. "You dragged a patient into our lives and now I can't stop thinking about her. And I keep thinking about her husband, putting up a bright front, trying to keep her alive with a party. I suppose he thinks she will die if they cancel. You too." She tilts her head and stares at Lawr, as if he were a painting she was trying to grasp from a new perspective. "Why else would you have told him to call me?"

151

"That's magical thinking," he says sternly. "Don't you know?"

"No. I don't know," she says, then tells him that as a child she wouldn't step on sidewalk cracks for fear something would happen to her mother, who knocked wood to ward off the evil eye whenever she mentioned the names of her children. Her grandmother wouldn't leave the house on Friday the 13th. Churlishly, Selma suggests that perhaps medical doctors are also in thrall to superstition.

And then she tells him how, not long ago, she discovered him standing at the bedroom mirror, a tube of lipstick in his hand. She stood just outside the room, holding her breath as he removed the cap and unrolled the lipstick from its silver tube. He put it up to the light, studying it with a curiosity he normally reserved for his plants. Then he poised it over his mouth, and Selma, who is not a religious woman, prayed. Was there was room in their life for this, whatever *this* was? In that moment she grasped how carefully she'd built her life around his, one assumption at a time, and that one false assumption could change everything. Like a sonata arranged in a new key, each note would have to be rearranged. When he capped the lipstick she thought her prayer had been answered, but then he slipped it in his pocket.

For weeks, Selma observed the way he touched her, wishing she'd had more experience with other men. She saw anew habits she hadn't noticed in years: his penchant for yellow ties; two sugars in his coffee; the way he crooked his pinky when he held tweezers to a mottled leaf. She scrutinized his mouth for stains in the places where her own lipstick tends to stray. She checked to see if her undergarments—arranged just so—had been disturbed.

"I was scared," she confesses, her voice strained and unnatural.

"I thought I didn't know you anymore. I wondered if I'd ever known you? Then at dinner one night, almost in passing, you mentioned that one of your nurses was leaving to teach a class at the hospital on the artful application of makeup. And I felt such a surge of relief." She recalls now, how he glumly noted that his nurse would be able to do more for his patients with a tube of lipstick than anything he could do with all the medicines at his disposal. "And just like that," she tells him, "our life returned to its original key and I exhaled."

Now looking across the table at her husband, she understands that she'd lied to herself. The musical notes, like her spoons and pots and pans, had changed. They'd become deeper, darker, more plaintive. They'd mellowed over time. Lawr, whom she has always loved for his willful determination, has become more of a sober realist. She is just beginning to understand how much she relies on his unbridled optimism, his faith in himself, which she sometimes feels extends to her. Now he has been trying to tell her that despite his best efforts, the elusive warbler is in further decline. His patient, too. And though he wouldn't agree, he has become a magical thinker, like her mother, like her grandmother, like herself. *Put on some lipstick; you'll feel better! Call Selma!*

"Here's the thing," she says. "I saw you put the lipstick in your pocket." She pauses and catches his gaze. "Why?"

He starts to speak, then stops, and she is left with one of his long silences.

"I need to know," she insists.

"My patients," he says, beginning to stumble and halt. "They think," he continues. "They think I'm a magician, that I have an endless supply of tricks up my sleeve."

"So you prescribe lipstick?" she asks, letting her voice go softer.

He shakes his head. "I wish I could."

She thinks about her own work. Once, a meringue fell apart on her, and now she knows never to bake one on a hot, humid day. "But you might," she says. "Use it. I saw you pocket it."

He tells her he almost used it on a patient, then got so frightfully dizzy he fled the room and threw it away. "Afterwards, I told myself, 'If this is really all you can offer you ought to be doing something else.'"

"You don't really want to be doing something else?" She eyes him warily, suddenly afraid of his reply. When he shakes his head, she leans back in her chair and playfully tells him that he'd taken her favorite lipstick. "You could have at least put it back." Then, because she has exposed him, she confesses her own transgression and tells him about Goldie's posh cream. "Anyway, it doesn't work," she says, with a shrug. "Kind of like those fancy pharmaceuticals you are beginning to doubt." She presses her squashy dewlaps. "See?"

"You look lovely," he says.

"Don't lie."

"It's true."

Suddenly shy, she averts her gaze and they sip their beer in silence.

When he reaches across the table and squeezes her hand, she looks up at him and considers his quiet, good looks, his expression fixed in a rueful smile. If she were a magician with a wild card up her sleeve, she would give it to him.

Tomorrow, she will return Goldie's cream, what's left of it. Then she'll call William and white lie that she can't take the job.

And she'll say, Hlavacek's. You can tell Mrs. Hlavacek that I sent you. She arranges lovely bouquets. That much is true.

Mr. Dalloway

WILLIAM HESITATES OUTSIDE THE BEDROOM DOOR, LIKE A long-legged wading bird standing frozen at the edge of a pond. He is clutching a spray of bougainvillea in one hand. The other, like an eager young suitor's, is poised to knock. What was it that Nora once called him? "My swain."

He pats his hair, his best feature. It is wiry and still thick, graying only at the temples. Then he fingers the knot in his tie. He has on the maroon bow tie with the gold fleur de lis, the one they bought two summers ago at the market in Florence.

The other day she remembered the tie. He'd gone to check on her before leaving for work. She spotted a missing button on his jacket. Then she said, "I've been thinking that your navy blue blazer would be just right for the party. And the bow tie from Florence. I'd love to see you in that."

He started to say that he'd love to see her in the blue silk dress she wore that day in the market, the one Mohammed the tie vendor said matched the signora's eyes. Then Maydell bustled in, piercing him with one of those sidelong fish-eyed looks of hers, and the moment was lost.

Now he presses his ear to the door and strains to catch what they are saying, but what he hears, sounds like nothing more than the low guttural cooing of roosting pigeons. Then there is a short burst of laughter. *Good,* he thinks. *This has been a good day. It is safe to knock.*

But what if Maydell is helping her slip into the blue silk dress? Perhaps Nora has declared that she feels well enough to come downstairs to help him greet the guests. He remembers how in his excitement he opened the wrong door on their wedding day and caught a glimpse of Nora, arms raised high above her head like an obedient child, waiting for her mother to lower the gown. "Bad luck," Mrs. Stern hissed as he fled. Yet they'd had good fortune for the most part. More than twenty-five years of it. In Florence, they'd even joked about returning to celebrate the next twenty-five. He promised to buy her golden earrings on the Ponte Vecchio. She promised to track down Mohammed. She bet that he'd still be selling ties, and if he were, William would owe her a golden necklace as well.

When he discovered the lump on her breast it was as if a third person had joined them in bed. "I'm sure it's nothing," she said. Though shouldn't he have been the reassuring one? Even now she's busy telling him everything will be all right. "You'll see, William," she said just the other day. "You'll manage fine without me. Look at the way you run your business." There was nothing disdainful in her remark. She meant it, just as she had when she told him to wear the Florentine tie to the party.

But he doesn't manage. Not really. He could have said, *Look at the way you run this house, or my life for that matter.* It is Nora who makes the dentist appointments, remembers his secretary's birthday, and knows which flowers to buy for parties. She would have known that a bougainvillea has thorns; that it will wilt before the first guests arrive. She'd even have stocked up on the toilet paper. He heard her say so to Maydell. "I hate to think of William rattling around the house, looking for toilet paper." He only caught part of Maydell's reply. "His own behind," she'd said, and he didn't know if he was hurt or shocked. Both really. Shocked by her insolence. She is, after all, a housekeeper whose status has been elevated out of necessity. He was hurt, too, that Nora hadn't rallied to his defense, though Maydell's incessant chattering could have drowned out her reply.

Maydell is angry with him for throwing a party. She is not afraid to remind him that his co-workers are the only people who have accepted his invitation. Old friends, relatives all declined. Ann's mother is angry, too. She even invited the rabbi over to speak with William. "To talk some sense into you," is how she put it.

William couldn't tell the rabbi why he is throwing a party when his wife is so ill. He didn't say that if he gives a party people won't know that he is afraid he won't remember when his teeth need cleaning or where to find the toilet paper in the supermarket. He didn't say that he is angry that he won't be able to honor a bet and buy his wife a string of golden beads.

He had reasoned that a party would cheer Nora up. Hadn't she rallied that time they'd gone out to dinner? She'd been resting all day, but after she got up, put on a new dress, pushed back her hair with a tortoise shell headband and put on some lipstick, she exclaimed, "This is better than a transfusion." Of course, after dinner, which ended before dessert, she went straight to bed.

But William didn't say any of that to the rabbi. He merely asked if there were any religious prohibitions against throwing a party during an illness. After the rabbi cleared his throat and plucked a piece of lint off his jacket sleeve, he suggested a support group. "Grief makes people do strange things," he intoned.

William had tried a group. The officious social worker at the cancer center assured him it would help. There were metal folding chairs arranged in a circle. A plate of Lorna Doone's was passed around. William sat between a woman with lymphoma and man whose wife was dying of lung cancer. There was a ketchup stain on the man's shirt, and he fought back tears as he talked about calling 911 to help get his wife out of the bathtub. Then a box of Kleenex went round the circle.

William never went back. He does his crying in private, standing at the kitchen sink with the water running, or stopped in traffic at a red light. Even that feels like too public a display of emotion, and he quickly dries his eyes with the back of his hand and checks the rear view mirror to see if anyone has noticed.

Now he checks his watch. Soon the first guests will arrive, and he's still standing, like some awkward stilt-legged bird outside his own bedroom door, hoping for nothing more than a wifely benediction before the party. *Knock,* he tells himself, then pictures Maydell cutting him down with those fish eyes of hers, mentally slamming the door in his face.

Moving to the guest room had been Nora's idea. "You'll sleep better," she'd said. But he heard her anyway, shuffling to the bathroom In the middle of the night, running bath water. He'd get up to tap on the door. "I'm fine, William," she'd call. "Go back to sleep." But he'd stand there until he heard water sloshing as she lifted herself up and the patter of footsteps across the tile floor.

Again he checks his watch, fingers the knot on his tie. In one minute he will open the door, present the flowers, apologize for the thorns. "You would have known better," he'll say. It's a fantasy, but he pictures her getting into the blue dress. Maydell will be standing there, waiting to zip it up. He will order her to step aside. *That's my job,* he'll say. Then he'll tell her to find something else to do. *Do the dishes. Mop the floor. Go home to that crack-dealing boyfriend of yours.*

When Maydell started ignoring the odd coffee cup in the kitchen sink, he didn't say anything. He even bit his tongue when he returned from work and found the breakfast dishes on the table or his bed unmade.

He is grateful for her help with Nora, for her unflinching competence. He, on the other hand, is awkward and clumsy around his wife, unable to fluff a pillow or hold a straw to her lips, without feeling as if she will expire under the weight of his ineptitude.

Maydell even bathes Nora. Once he walked in on them while she was sudsing Nora's hair. Nora's eyes were closed, her face serene as she surrendered to the pleasures of touch. "Ummm. That feels good," she sighed. How many times had she said that to him as he stood behind her in the shower, pressing into her as he soaped her back or lathered her hair? And when he turned her around to work the shampoo into the patch between her legs, she didn't have to tell him how good it felt. Now he sees fear in her eyes whenever he comes near. Is she afraid he'll hurt her with his clumsy gestures? Or is she saying something else? *I don't want you to see me like this.*

Now, Maydell's voice is rising and again he presses his ear to the door. The other day he overheard her saying, "You'll never guess what Mr. William's done now." Then she told Nora about the cheese-cakes. "All the way from New York City. Like there ain't no place in Chicago that sells those. And the flowers. Something I never heard of. Something with a *b*."

"Bougainvillea," Nora replied. When she said, "My favorite," he felt his shoulders relax. But then she said, "So Mr. Dalloway is buy-ing the flowers himself." Maydell must have given her one of those looks, because Nora told her about the book, about Mrs. Dalloway's feverish preparation and her determination to buy the flowers for the party herself.

The next day a worn copy of *Mrs. Dalloway* appeared on the crowded nightstand alongside the pills, the lotions, the water glass, the shocking pink lipstick Nora always wore. She asked him to hand her the lipstick but refused his offer to fetch a mirror. "If I don't know the shape of my own lips by now, William, I never will."

I know it, too, he almost blurted. He wanted to press his mouth to hers, taste the waxy perfume, feel his lips bruised the color of crushed flower petals. *Once more,* he thought, realizing he couldn't remember the last time they'd kissed, or made love. If only he'd known, he might have made a mental note to mark the occasion. But he didn't say any of that. Instead he offered to read from the book.

"Some other time," she murmured, as she settled back into the pile of pillows and closed her eyes. Later, he heard Maydell stum-bling over the flawless prose. "Go home and sing rap," he muttered as he turned away. It was an unfair remark, for he knows Maydell sings in her church choir while wearing a red robe to signify the blood of Christ, and silver shoes to signify her own earthly desires. She has a beautiful voice.

Now voices flare in the kitchen as a dish shatters. In their haste, the caterers are getting careless. It is time to knock. But first, he holds the flowers to his nose and is surprised they have no scent. He should have thought of that. Yet nothing will mask the death smell of his wife. Not the flowers. Not the lemony ointment Maydell rubs on Nora's lips, or the chamomile tea that sits untouched on the nightstand. Not the alcohol, or Lysol, or Maydell's lavender-scented hand cream.

"Now," he says. "Knock now." But how? Their voices will drown out a simple tap.

Rat a tat tat seems too playful.

Knock. Knock. Too tentative.

Cha. Cha. Cha. That could work. Perhaps Nora will recall the trophy they won the year she roped him into ballroom dancing lessons. He'd balked. She prevailed. She was right; it was fun. She's always right. Cha. Cha. Cha. Of course she'll recall. After all, she remembered the tie.

Last Wish

SINCE THE ARRIVAL OF THE INVITATION, HARRY AND CLARA, the Olympic Champions of bickering, have been fighting even more. Then after reading how the placement of furniture affects a household's peace and harmony, she moved the dresser. All these years she'd blamed their troubles on Harry's temper, when the problem, it seemed, was nothing more than a careless misalignment of the furniture.

Nevertheless, while Clara is in the kitchen fixing breakfast and packing Harry's lunch, that temper erupts in a keening howl. You'd think someone had died, though this outburst could have been triggered by nothing more than a search for a matching pair of socks.

She is cutting across the diagonal of two slices of rye when Harry appears. Her back is to him while she wraps his sandwich in waxed paper and listens for the familiar sounds: the scrape of his chair against the polished linoleum; the rustle of newspaper as he punches it open. "And good morning to you, too," she says, without turning.

By way of reply he says, "For twenty-seven years the chifforobe stays in one place. Helen Keller could find her way in that room without a cane. Then Mrs. Allied Van Lines has to go and move it. And I stub my toe."

She takes her time with the finishing touches: an apple, three Grandfather seed cookies, a paper napkin folded, also on the diagonal. Let him wait for his coffee. His oatmeal. With brown sugar and raisins. The way he likes it. For nearly forty years, almost twice as many as they've owned the dresser, Clara has been serving his breakfast like one of those good-natured waitresses at Sam & Hy's. She doesn't mind. He works hard all day, slicing and weighing meat, keeping up a cheery banter with his customers, every one of them insisting on the choicest cut. Standing behind a meat counter is Harry's job. Taking care of him is hers. Still.

She sets his lunch near the coat rack before turning to him. He's built like a buffalo, short and broad, though not any more so than the day they'd met. Now he combs his thinning hair over the top, carefully distributing each strand to compensate for what's missing. Dark pouches have pooled beneath his eyes. His jowls have succumbed to gravity. But years of hauling sides of beef have kept him fit. He is wearing a blue knit shirt and the brown trousers she'd pressed last night. When he gets to the shop, he'll slip into work clothes and a fresh white smock. He's a proud man.

"Let me have a look," she says.

Without glancing up, he stabs the newspaper with a stubby finger, the one he sliced to the knuckle years ago, and the one which, last night, had gently caressed her breasts. It amazes her that such familiar territory doesn't bore him. And she hasn't tired of the routine.

Now, with that truncated finger he points to a picture of a young girl who blew herself up in a crowded Tel Aviv market. Eighteen souls died along with her.

"Not the news," Clara sighs. She's read the paper. Suicide bombers. Melting ice caps. Bees dying off, and nobody knows why. Bats, too. Monarch butterflies. She's in no mood to engage with Harry about any of that, or about his stubbed toe, for that matter.

She'd wanted to talk about William's party. *He cried, Harry. That's what she'd planned to say. He stood at the kitchen sink and cried.* But the moment has passed. Besides, Harry wouldn't understand, just like he wouldn't fathom her reasons for moving the chifforobe. *You're crazy,* he'd say. She's sorry she ever picked up that magazine with its clever household tips. She's sorry, too, that she hadn't wedged that chest of drawers between their beds, which have been seamlessly joined together all these years.

She collapses into the chair beside him and repeats that she's seen the news. "Your toe," she says, looking down at his foot. "I thought maybe you'd show me your toe."

He drags his right foot out from under the table and stomps it, leaving a broad scuffmark on the freshly waxed floor.

"If you can do that," she says, "it can't be so bad."

"Easy for you to say. You didn't run into the chifforobe."

When she asks if it bled, he buries his nose in the paper.

She pushes herself out of the chair and makes her way to the stove to stir the oatmeal. She wonders if he's reading the story about the mother who told the judge that God had ordered her to kill her children? Then she wonders what would happen if she were to lie and tell everyone in this interfering family of hers that God had

167

instructed her to attend William's party? You'd think she was planning to hold a child's head under the bath water until his face turned blue. Or strap a bomb to her midriff and blow herself up in a market crowded with shoppers.

She sets his oatmeal before him. "I asked you a question, Harry."

"What's that?" he says, glancing up from the paper.

"Your toe. Did it bleed?"

"It throbbed," he says, and before she can stop him, he yanks off his loafer and starts taking off his sock. "Here! Take a good look, Miss Florence Nightingale," he says, thrusting his foot in the air.

Wearily, she tells him to put his shoe back on. "You'll be late to work," she says and pours his coffee.

After jamming his foot back in the shoe, he says, "And just what do you plan to do all day while I'm at work?"

She wonders if he'll ever acknowledge that she works as a dressmaker at home. "I'm going to move the chifforobe back," she says, settling into her chair.

He nods approvingly. "Wait until I get home," he says. "Please. I don't want you moving it alone."

She spreads a thin layer of marmalade on a piece of stone cold toast. "Whatever you say."

"Whatever I say?" His eyes light up. His voice assumes an unexpected lilt. "Does that mean you won't be going to that cockamamie party tonight?"

Briefly, she closes her eyes and imagines herself already standing in the Hill's living room, wearing her navy blue shirtwaist with white polka dots. Polka dots, being neither festive nor somber, seemed just right for an occasion for which she could find no precedent.

"You're going, aren't you," says Harry, his voice jerking her back to the fractious present.

She hasn't made up her mind. Yesterday, she'd gone to William, hoping he might say or do something to help her decide. It wasn't like Clara not to phone ahead, but she'd wanted to surprise him. Catch him off guard. She'd told herself that if she found him in the kitchen crying over the sink, like the last time she'd visited, she would go to the party. But if she caught him whistling Broadway show tunes as he unpacked the groceries—she imagined flowers, wine, crusty baguettes—her dress would go right back in the closet.

Instead of William, Clara got Maydell, the young woman who used to clean house and now also looks after Nora. Clara stood on the doorstep holding out a pan of kugel, her standard offering when visiting the grieving or sick. When she asked if William was at home, Maydell whipped her head around, then whipped it back, the colorful beads that held her tight braids in place clicking like tiny castanets. "Nope. I guess not," she said, as she took the kugel from Clara's outstretched arms. "He's probably out shopping for that party of his. Says he going to get the flowers his self. Poor Miss Nora. She goes and buys all that toilet paper when she still feeling well enough to be out and about. One day she comes home and says how she don't want Mr. William rattling round the house after she gone, looking for toilet paper." Maydell paused, her surprising blue eyes fixed on Clara. "You think he don't know how to get to the Jewel and buy it his self?"

Clara tried recalling whether Harry had ever been to the Jewel. Though it was a warm fall day, she pulled her cardigan tighter around her ample bosom at the thought of Harry pushing a cart up and down the aisles in search of toilet paper.

"It's a wonder that man can wipe his own behind," Maydell bristled. "Now he be gallavantin' all over town, buying this and that for that party of his."

Clara stood for a long moment and when she found her voice she instructed Maydell to refrigerate the kugel. "Before serving," she said, "just warm it in a slow oven."

✻ ✻ ✻

It is a cheerless party, which oddly comforts Clara, who went intending not to enjoy herself. By the time the taxi picked her up (she wouldn't dream of asking Harry to drive her), she had changed three times until she was in polka dots.

By the time she arrives, twenty or so of William's co-workers are milling around the living room and spilling over into other rooms of the meandering house. They're young by Clara's standards—late thirties, early forties, she guesses. Some of the women are sinking into middle-aged softness. The men show signs of collapse around the middle. What are they to William? Secretaries? Computer programmers? Do they know about Nora? If they had known, would they have declined the invitation, like Edith and Harry and the rest of the family? The boycott was Edith's doing. Harry's sister loves to stir things up.

The day the invitation arrived Edith phoned all worked up about a "cheap little Hallmark card." Clara had been basting the hem of a mother-of-the-bride dress—a confection of apricot chiffon with a ballerina hemline.

"What are you talking about?" she'd ask, impatient to get back to work.

"The invitation," Edith snapped.

"What invitation?"

"Do me a favor," Edith said. "Hang up the phone. Go check your mail. Then call me back."

When Clara called back, Edith said, "I've already responded. That *schvartze* girl answered the phone. I said, 'Tell Mr. Hill, thank you very much, but no thank you.'"

Later that day, Edith called to report that William had asked Selma Marks, the doctor's wife, to cater the party. "That's one for the Guinness Book of Records," he said, though it wasn't clear what record had been broken. As it turned out, Selma had a previous booking.

Clara considered taking the phone off the hook, but Harry would have a fit if he couldn't get through. He never called. Edith did, this time with news that Harry wasn't going to the party, either.

"What do you mean, Harry isn't going?" Clara said, rather crossly.

"I stopped by the shop to pick up a little something for dinner," Edith explained.

Clara could picture her sister-in-law, straight from her mid-week comb-out at Mr. Jon's, standing in front of Harry's meat counter waving the invitation in the air as she ordered a single lamb chop.

Now, alone among strangers at a party she did not want to attend, Clara casts an eye over the Hill's living room, searching for a face. The guests are clustered in impenetrable knots, chattering like mynah birds, tossing their heads back and laughing, gingerly balancing wine glasses and plates, peering over shoulders for someone possibly more interesting to appear.

There's William! He's weaving through the room refreshing wine glasses. How had she missed him in those brilliant slacks? They're the kind favored by golfers, though if he were ever to swing a club, he'd cause considerable damage. "A bull in a china closet," Edith calls him, though in truth he resembles a gangly wading bird.

The family has always thought Nora could have done better, but William has been kind to Clara. When she started her sewing business, he helped set up the books. And he never fails to ask how things are going. He's a klutz, his own worst enemy, always seeming to trip over those long, double-jointed limbs. He's one of those people who apologize for their very existence. But he bore no ill will. He certainly hadn't caused Nora's cancer, though Clara knows the family holds that against him, too.

The doorbell chimes. It's the rabbi. William greets him, takes the man's coat. Shortly after the invitations went out, Nora's mother recruited the rabbi to talk some sense into William. Then she and the others turned on the rabbi, too. Perhaps he is here to importune William one last time. Clara imagines him moving to the center of room, stand on tiptoe—he is short and his voice is surprisingly weak for a spiritual leader—to announce, that under the circumstances, the party is being called off. Instead, he trudges up the stairs, shoulders stooped, head bowed, like a man who knows that whatever prayers he is about to invoke will go unanswered.

The last time Clara had been upstairs, Nora was out of bed. Maydell had propped her up in a red leather chair, the pillows stuffed around her to keep her from flopping over. "It's all right, Clara. You can come in," Nora rasped. At first, Clara had trouble connected the weak voice to the swaddled figure in the chair. Then her eyes adjusted, the way they accommodate from light to dark, and she could see, beneath the wreckage, a glimmer of the green-eyed beauty with abundant auburn hair. If only Clara had been forewarned. She might have rehearsed an expression in which shock and fear were not written all over her face. At the very least, she could have willed herself to march right up to Nora and plant a kiss on cheek. Instead, she'd hung back, shrinking into the doorpost, recoiling from the apparition in front of her.

Clara had doted on both Nora and her sister Vivian. When the girls were younger she sewed for them, the way she would have, if she'd had children of her own. She stitched seersucker rompers, plaid schoolgirl jumpers, pleated skirts, Polly Flinders knock-offs with hand smocking. She sewed Nora's wedding dress. Nora posed for fittings, standing barefooted on the shag carpeting while Clara whipped a tape measure around her slender frame. When Clara draped a length of the shimmering white fabric diagonally across Nora's chest—the part that would become her undoing—she might have been adjusting a sash on a beauty queen. "I look as if I've been gift wrapped," Nora had laughed, when Clara turned her to face the mirror. "You look beautiful," Clara beamed.

William had been in the kitchen playing solitaire when Clara returned downstairs. He'd looked up from the cards, his face twisted with fear. "How was she?" he whispered.

"She was sitting up. In the red chair," Clara replied, the only truth she cared to convey.

"You're one of her favorites," he'd said.

"And she's one of mine." Clara managed a smile. "My favorite niece-once-removed." Technically they weren't related. Nora's mother was a sister of Edith's husband. Clara and Nora had settled on the kinship term years ago, during a fitting for the wedding gown.

William had asked Clara to stay for tea. When she offered to prepare it, he said, "If I can't boil water, I'll be in trouble."

He stood at the sink and let the water run long after the kettle was full. Water overflowed from its spout splashing his shirtfront, the wall, the counter, even the floor. And still, he didn't turn it off.

Clara, who had been searching for knife to cut the kugel, ordered him to sit.

"No. You sit," he said. Then, with the water still running, he dropped the kettle into the sink, gripped the edge of the counter and leaned over, his shoulders trembling. "I can't stand seeing her like this," he mumbled. A long minute passed. Then abruptly, he straightened up and wiped his eyes with the back of his hand. "I don't know what's come over me," he said, with an apologetic smile.

"It's all right, William." She turned off the tap, patted his back and led him to the table. Then she rummaged through the cabinets for tea, feeling like the kind of guest who snoops in the host's medicine cabinet, though she unearthed no secrets, unless dearth is something to hide. One can of soup. A half-empty bag of rice. Corn Flakes. True, one shelf was crammed with spices for Indian dinners Nora loved to prepare, but one rarely runs out of those.

"There's green tea somewhere," William said, when Clara pulled out a box of Lipton's. "Someone gave it to Nora early on." He paused, lowered his gaze. "Everyone had the magic cure."

A flush crept up Clara's neck as she recalled mixing raisins into the kugel, thinking the iron would be good for Nora.

"We have it all, Clara. Meditation tapes. Soy cookbooks. Copper bracelets." He let out a wild laugh, then honked his nose into a paper napkin. "Green tea. I'm sure we have some."

"This is good enough," Clara said, dropping two teabags into a pair of mugs. "Harry and I have a cup of Lipton's every night after dinner." Instantly, she regretted the reference to the kind of intimacy that William would soon be denied. What patterns had he and Nora fallen into over the years? They were younger than Harry and Clara, a different generation altogether, but twenty-five years is long enough to inhabit a routine. Perhaps she could offer that living with Harry was no picnic, as if the death of a spouse might have a bright side. She could reveal that Harry pounded the table when he was angry, until the cups jumped away from the saucers.

She set a mug before him. "Drink this," she urged. "You'll feel better."

He stared down at his tea. "I read somewhere . . ." He stopped abruptly, looked up and fixed her with his considerate gaze, as if waiting for her to tell him what he had read. After a long silence, he said, "Did you know that the average life of a botanist is 68.3 years? Entomologists live beyond 70. And British authors and poets live to 63.9." He shook his head and smiled ruefully. "Who calculates such things? And how?" He paused. "Nora," he said. "I suppose she brings the averages way down."

Just then Maydell appeared, her strong, dark arms enfolding a load of bed linens. William set down his mug, half rose from his chair, and if Clara wasn't mistaken, he bent at the waist as the young woman passed through on her way to the basement.

Clara never told Harry any of this. Not even when he accused her of being a traitor, after she announced her decision. "Mrs. Benedict Arnold," he'd called her. Even then she didn't tell him how William forgot to eat his kugel, or that the cabinets were bare, or that

175

William had bowed to the maid. And she certainly didn't reveal that he'd silently wept over the sink. The man deserved his privacy.

And so Harry had bellowed: "What kind of man throws a party when his wife is dying?" A scared man, Clara had wanted to say. *He stood at the sink and cried.* But then Harry would offer something about poor Mr. Crybaby. He'd remind her that William was not the one who was dying. Though technically correct, he'd be wrong.

❋ ❋ ❋

As the rabbi retreats up the stairs, Clara, adrift, contemplates the milling guests. Their knots have grown tighter, more impenetrable. She decides to eat.

It's a generous spread, albeit perfunctory: cold cuts fanned out over a bed of curly kale; canned pineapple in the fruit salad; packaged rye. The desserts on the sideboard bring to mind Edith phoning to say that William was flying in cheesecakes from New York. "A Chicago bakery isn't good enough?" she'd sniffed. Clara agreed that the man had gone overboard. "A megalomaniac," Edith said. "That too," Clara replied, not wanting to appear disagreeable.

Now regarding those cakes she wonders if Edith had a point. Then she sees the flowers—yellow carnations with tightly-permed faces. She recalls Nora's whimsical centerpieces. Geraniums in rustic clay pots. Pink rose buds floating in crystal pools of water. At this time of year she would have done something playful with baby pumpkins, bittersweet, an abundance of mums. Clara turns away from the stingy carnations. No matter how many cheesecakes he imports, William will never get things right. He is destined, she fears, to haplessly wander the grocery store aisles.

She feels deflated, like the stale drink with melting ice cubes someone has thoughtlessly left on the buffet table. She removes the glass and makes a beeline for the kitchen. She will call Harry. She hasn't the will to make small talk with a taxi driver, or worse, endure the cab ride home in palpable silence. Harry will have to pick her up. When they get home, they will move the chifforobe. Then they'll settle into bed like a pair of nesting spoons, his steady breath warming the back of her neck as she drifts to sleep.

William is in the kitchen, elbows propped on the table, head resting in his hands. Two platters of cold cuts are spread out before him. He'd been expecting a crowd. "I thought she'd rally," he says, looking up at Clara with a helpless shrug. "I could picture her descending the staircase in her blue silk dress."

Clara nods. She once read about a ten-year-old boy with leukemia who had never been to a major league baseball game. A group that grants wishes to dying children flew him from Cedar Rapids to Chicago. They boy sat in the Cubs' dugout, shook Sammy Sosa's hand, got autographed pictures of the team.

Perhaps survivors should be granted a wish, too. But would they ever be satisfied? If Nora were to grace the party in blue silk, William might want to take the trip to France they'd been planning before the cancer returned. He might want one more evening at their favorite restaurant. One more night making love.

She tries picturing Harry swaddled like an infant in a red leather chair. If it comes to that, will she wish for him to rattle the teacups, just one more time? Or rant over a missing sock? She reaches across the table and takes William's hand. "Nora can't come down," she says. He lifts his head, confusion clouding his face, as if she has

177

told him something new and unfathomable: there is no tooth fairy, no Santa Claus.

"But you can go upstairs." She pats his hand. Again, he regards her with confusion. "Go," she whispers. "Be with your wife."

"The guests," he murmurs.

"I'll take care of the guests," she assures him.

He nods, but remains seated, like a polite child waiting to be excused from the table. "It's all right," she says. "Go."

He pulls away from the table with uncustomary grace, managing to unfold his awkward frame without upsetting the platters of food.

Clara returns to the party. She moves to the center of the living room and lightly taps a spoon to the rim of a lipstick-stained glass. The room falls still; the guests lean in expectantly. Somebody coughs. Someone else clears his throat. The spoon slips from Clara's hand and there is nervous laughter as she bends to retrieve it. Again, she raises the glass, this time as if she means to offer a toast. When she can trust her voice, she says, "William had to leave the party early. He asked me to tell you." She falters. He hadn't asked her to say anything. She recalls the table laden with food; the imported cakes. He is a generous man. Misguided, but generous. She manages to continue. "Stay," she says, her voice unsure. Then with greater conviction she adds, "That's what William asked me to tell you. He wants you to stay." They lean closer in, expecting more. "Oh, yes. And he says to have a good time." She raises the empty glass and offers a toast. *"L'chaim!"*

In the kitchen, she washes and dries the glass and spoon. After putting them away, she phones Harry, who answers on the first ring. "Come and get me," she says.

ABOUT THE AUTHOR

MIRIAM KARMEL GREW UP IN CHICAGO. SHE IS THE author of *Being Esther: A Novel* (Milkweed Editions, 2013). She received *Minnesota Monthly*'s Tamarack Award for her short story, "The Queen of Love." Other awards for her short fiction include the Waasnode Prize, the Kate Braverman Prize, and the *Moment Magazine*/Karma Foundation Prize. *Subtle Variations and Other Stories* is the recipient of the inaugural "First Fiction" Prize from Holy Cow! Press. She lives in Minneapolis, Minnesota.